THE WARBIRDS

THE WARBIRDS

E.C. TUBB

First published as *Saturn Patrol*

WILDSIDE PRESS

CHAPTER I

THE WARBIRD

The ship stood like a dirty finger, poised on the landing field at the edge of town. Once sleek sides were marked and scarred, stained with tarnish and mottled with poorly applied patches. One fin was twisted, and the plastic of ports and turrets clouded with flight strain and neglect. Yet, despite the general air of decay, something of the original beauty still showed. The clean, utilitarian lines of a perfect machine in the long curves, the subtle swellings of the venturis could still be seen.

Gregg Harmond, who had once aspired to pilot a spaceship in the now defunct Space Patrol, could see it. He thought now: "It's the loveliest thing ever made."

He stood against the edge of the field, head tilted back, eyes half-closed against the whirling snow. Wind whipped at his tall, fur-clad form, biting savagely at exposed cheeks and throat, sending the warming numbness of frostbite. He sighed and turned away. A smaller figure, blurred in the snow, came stumbling towards him.

"Gregg!"

"Yes? Oh—it's you, Owen."

"I've been looking for you." The small, fur-bundled shape fell into step with him. "Did you see it?"

"Yes. It's a ship all right. First in two years. What do the elders say?"

"They don't like it. It's got to leave tomorrow."

"Are you sure?"

"I heard my father talking to the others. They are afraid of it, but they had to let it land for water."

"I see." He laughed curtly. "No wonder they kept it so quiet. They say anything else?"

"I didn't hear," Owen confessed. "I came out to see the ship."

They walked for a time in silence, picking their way over the rough, snow-covered road leaving into town. Night had fallen, and from the frozen pole a bitter wind thrust at their bodies.

Owen shivered. "Are you going with it, Gregg?"

"Maybe. Why?" He was deliberately curt.

"If you go, can I come with you?"

Harmond stopped, staring down at the indistinct shape. "That's impossible."

"But why, Gregg? I'm over eighteen. Jeff Trammond said he was going and he's not much older than I am."

"Jeff Trammond talks too much. What about your father? What about Jean?"

"Oh, Jean." Owen shrugged with the careless indifference of a brother. "She won't mind."

"And your father?" Gregg asked dryly.

"He won't know," said Owen simply.

Harmond sighed and began walking towards the signal beacon ahead.

"Look, Owen," he said gently, "You don't know what you're asking. For me, it's different. Ever since my folks died, I've wanted to get away from here. With the last crop failure, I expect to lose the section through default, and I don't want to work for hire. But your father is an Elder. You've got everything to lose by going. Why not be sensible?"

"I want to go with you, Gregg."

"But I don't want you, Owen," he mimicked angrily.

"Why, Gregg?"

"Because it's a Warbird," he answered savagely. "That's why."

They walked on in silence.

* * * *

He sat in the tavern on the edge of town, a big man, jolly, filling the place with his roaring songs and shouts of mirth. Shimmering cellosilk, cunningly cut, disguised his gross bulk. A wide belt supported a heavy blaster resting against one thick thigh, and though the belt looked new, the weapon was not.

He was free with his money, calling for round after round of the fiery local brew, tossing gold coins down the low-cut dresses of the girls, grinning at their delighted squeals.

Around him, listening to his vain-glorious boasting, drinking his wine, cheering his songs, stood the youth of the town. Working men mostly. Hired hands, with a scattering of small section holders. Hard workers, their dirt-stained fingers twitched with faint avarice and half-hidden envy. Standing back from the crowd stood the Elders. Old men, the wealthy, the rulers of the town. They gathered into little groups, talking among themselves, frowning at the big stranger.

He drained his pot and set it down with a bang.

"Drink up, my hearties. Drink, and bless the day the Warbirds landed here. Look at me—a drink for my friends, silk on my back, not a stroke of labour in a twelvemonth, and this belly never came from starving." He patted his bulk while the youths drew nearer.

"It's a fine life, I tell you. A free life and a merry one. None of your grubbing in the soil, freezing in this cursed wind, starving when the crops fail. A spell on watch, a ship in your sights, a squeeze of a finger, and the loot of a world for the taking."

One of the Elders stepped forward, his eyes glinting angrily. "Have a care, Captain. We permitted you to land on the understanding that you would keep to your ship and do no recruiting. You will remember that, if you please."

"So?" The big man almost hissed the word. "It's keep to your ship, is it?"

One hand dropped almost idly to the heavy blaster. "You scream for us quick enough when your pockets are in danger, but in the fat days it's 'keep to your ship'. What are you afraid of? Afraid that some of your tame cattle here will take wing? Afraid that we will poison your air?"

Anger darkened his features. "Commander Alendi lies in his bunk a sick man. Any other planet would have been pleased to entertain us, but you people on the Rim are all the same. Cowards, the lot of you!"

An ugly murmur sounded from the group around him. He ignored it.

"I know what's in your mind," he told the Elder. "I tell you now I'm not going. Just try and make me. Just try."

The Elder stared at him for a moment; whatever his faults he was no coward, but he was old. Against an armed man, a ruthless man, he was helpless, but the glint in his eyes boded ill for the fat Captain. Gregg stood just within the door loosening his furs, taking in the scene. He had no love for the Elders, but they were his people. With one quick movement, he stood against the stranger; another, and he had the blaster resting easily in his hand.

"Apologise," he said curtly.

"What?"

"Apologise. You'll be dead if you don't," Gregg said dully. "He's an old man, unarmed. Apologise."

For a moment their eyes locked, then the gross bulk of the man shook with silent laughter. "By Space, but you're a hard one! As you say then, my apologies to you, sir, and a drink all round."

He held out his hand. "My weapon, please."

Gregg shook his head. "I'll give it to you later. It may go off—by accident."

More laughter shook the fat frame. "Merry's the name. Captain of the ship out yonder. Pleased to meet at last one man who can claim to that title."

"Harmond. Gregg Harmond. I want to ship with you."

"Eh?" Merry stared in amazement. "After what you've just done, the best place for you is the other side of the Galaxy!" He grew thoughtful. "Any others of your kidney around?"

Gregg shrugged, not answering.

"Ten credits a day. Free food and weapons. Sign on for the duration, and a bonus at the end of it. We're a strong group. Plenty of pickings with Alendis Undefeateds. What say you?"

His words, with Harmond's example, fired some of the waverers. Several surged forward to fix their thumb print onto the articles of attestation. The Elders looked on, glowering. One of them stepped forward.

"I know you, Harmond. A shiftless worker. Lagos is well rid of you. Owen," he snapped sharply, "home."

For a moment, indecision showed on the chubby features then Owen sighed and struggled into his furs.

"Good luck, Gregg," he called. The door slammed behind him.

Merry grinned lopsidedly. "All right men. Assemble on the field at dawn. Fifty kilos of personal kit each, no more."

He turned to Gregg. "Now, shipmate, where's my blaster?"

He took the outstretched weapon, hefted it in one huge paw, then with sudden casual viciousness smashed it against the side of Harmond's head. Again and again.

Merry stared down at the huddled figure at his feet. Deliberately he spat.

* * * *

Harmond groaned, lifted his head and retched in sudden nausea. He was lying on a narrow bunk, covered by a single blanket, and his naked skin crawled at the touch of the sleazy covering. Stained bulkheads, rivet-studded, walled him in, and by the quivering of the bunk he knew the ship was blasting.

Acceleration weighed him down, the blood pounding through his battered skull. He blacked out.

When next he opened his eyes, Merry stood over him. The fat man no longer wore the shimmering cellosilk with which he had dazzled the youth of Lagos. The blaster still rested against one thigh, though supported by a less ornate belt.

He spat at Harmond. "Get up!"

"My—head—I..."

"Get up, I said." He laughed callously. "Your head hurts, does it? Well, well. Maybe I can cure that for you." Deliberately he lifted his huge paw, closed it into a fist, and sent the fist arching forward. It never landed.

Gregg left the cot in one swift motion, all pain and nausea burned away by the fierce anger which filled him. He stepped forward, ducked, straightened and struck. Merry roared with pain and anger, a rivulet of blood trickling from one corner of his mouth. Spitting out a mouthful of blood, he met the next rush with cold brutality. Shaken, Gregg staggered back, pain bringing delayed caution.

He couldn't hope to win. He was in poor condition, still dizzy and sick from his previous beating. Merry was a mass of hard flesh and muscle, in perfect condition, and in his element. As the fat man came towards him, Gregg looked round desperately. Nothing, the room as bare but for the single blanket on the cot. With a swift scooping motion, Gregg gathered it up, and flung it at Merry's head.

For a moment the man was blinded beneath the greasy folds; it was enough. Gregg stepped back, the blaster heavy in his hand, a cold smile on his lips.

"Easy, Merry. Easy or I'll burn your guts out."

"What?" Merry grabbed at his empty holster. "Why, you scum! Give me that blaster."

"Am I that crazy? Look what happened the last time."

Merry made no answer. To Gregg's surprise, he began advancing purposely forward, one hand outstretched. "That's the second time you've disarmed me, bucko. You know what happened the first time. Now I'm going to kill you."

"I think not," said Gregg contemptuously. "This time I keep it, and use it if I have to."

The fat man made no reply. He still came forward, a dogged look of defiance on his gross features. Alarmed, Gregg lifted the weapon, sighted on the bulging stomach, and tightened his finger.

He couldn't do it!

Something of what he felt must have showed in his face, for with a shout of triumph, Merry leapt forward.

With the desperation of despair, Gregg swung the heavy gun, smashing at the florid face before him. His arm was swept aside, the next moment he crumpled in the thick arms.

Frantically he used his knees, elbows, chopped with his hands, stabbed with his stiffened fingers. He did damage, the grunts and curses told him that, but he was receiving as good as he gave.

Finally, his overtaxed strength exhausted, he gave up. Merry had his thick hands around his throat and slowly began to throttle him.

"You're a fool," he grunted, "and a fool must pay for his folly. You've got guts, and that I like. But you're still a fool. Why didn't you use the blaster?"

Gregg gurgled, and Merry eased the pressure. "Go to hell, you fat slob!"

"Not," said Merry, tightening his grasp, "that it would have made any difference. I'm not a fool if you are. The blaster wasn't loaded, but of course you couldn't know that."

Surprisingly he laughed, and stepped back.

Half-throttled, Gregg reeled against the bulkhead and stared at him in wonder. Merry pulled a flat bottle from his hip pocket and handed it over.

"Here. Drink heavy, shipmate, and no ill feelings."

He watched while Gregg took a cautious sip, then a deep swallow. "Thanks."

"You've a lot to learn yet, Harmond, but I'll teach you. I've followed the Eagles for over thirty years, and I know it all, but nobody disarms me and insults me without paying for it. It was a lesson you had to learn."

He reached for the bottle.

"I'm glad that you're not yellow, but I wish that you had used the blaster."

"Why?" Gregg asked curiously.

"Never give an enemy a chance. Remember that. It's always him or you, and the quicker you learn that the longer you'll live." He sighed. "There's no place for chivalry in the Warbirds."

A noise from the still open door interrupted Gregg's reply. He stared in shocked disbelief.

"Owen! What are you doing here?"

"Hello, Gregg." Owen had the grace to look ashamed. "I couldn't stay behind when I knew you were going, so I ran away. I'm gallery boy," he announced with youthful pride, "serving the Commander himself."

"You fool!" Gregg was bitter. "Now Jean will blame me, your father too." He turned to Merry. "You can't take him. His father is an Elder of Lagos. If you ever intend going back there, you'd better return his son."

Merry shrugged. "He's of age. The articles are signed. He's a crewmember for the duration, and there's no going back."

He spoke to the boy, "What was it, son?"

"Commander Alendi's compliments, sir, and you are requested to attend general assembly on the mess room." Surprisingly he saluted; to Gregg the action looked utterly ridiculous.

Merry returned the gesture, a twinkle in his eye. "Thank you. We'll be right along." He chuckled at Gregg's stare.

"Surprised? Wait 'til you see Alendi. Better get dressed now; your uniform is under the cot."

It was rough, nothing like the cellosilk Merry had worn, but it fitted as well as could be expected, and once dressed Gregg felt a lot better. He followed the fat Captain as he led the way through the instrument-cluttered ship, and Gregg looked about him with interest.

It was not a new ship. It wasn't even a clean one. Many of the bulkheads bore the signs of hard usage, scarred, patched and twisted with strain. Bright metal work was tarnished and dull. Plastic covers of instrument cases were chipped and broken, in some cases missing entirely. The whole interior of the vessel was coated with what seemed a thick layer of greasy dust. Merry noticed his surprised stare.

"We've always been short-handed," he explained. "Too busy for cleaning. That grease is from the guns; the turrets aren't as tight as they should be and some of the back-flash escapes into the ship." He chuckled. "I've known the time when it was hard to see your own faceplate."

Gregg frowned. "But isn't it dangerous? To work a ship in this condition, I mean."

"Dangerous! Of course it's dangerous, but what can we do? We can't get money without work, and can't get work without a ship." He sighed. "Maybe with a different Commander. But Alendi's getting old and doesn't care too much as long as the bridge is clean."

He ducked through a low doorway, and Gregg saw that they had entered the mess room. About thirty men lounged in various attitudes. Some of them he recognized as those who had joined them. They looked disgruntled and angry, gathered together in a tight knot, glowering at those around them.

He was about to speak when a furtive-eyed, stooped little man yelled a command, and stood rigid.

"Attention!"

Gregg smiled, looked up, and saw Alendi.

CHAPTER 2

ALENDI

He stood just within the room. A tall, thin man, slightly stooped with age, impeccably dressed in a uniform heavy with insignia. Thin white hair receded from a scholar's forehead. Black eyes burned in a long, thin paper whiteness. Deep grooves ran from nostrils to the corners of a down-turned mouth.

He stood silently watching, and with him watched the thousand year ghost of olden Grandees. Pride! It radiated from the slight figure. Pride of command. Pride of birth. Pride of achievement. He was almost insane with sheer, blinding pride!

He made a gesture to the furtive-eyed man.

"At ease!" yelled that individual, and slumped to a more comfortable position. The others had moved not at all. Watching, Gregg felt a tinge of pity. The old Commander spoke.

"Men." His voice was barely a whisper, yet penetrated to every ear. "As is my custom with all new recruits, I welcome you to the glorious ranks of the Eagles. Some of you know what we are, what we stand for. To those, what I have to say will not be new. To you others, to those of you who are making their first flight under the brave standard of that mighty Warbird of old, the Eagle, I give welcome." The thin voice paused. A rustle ran throughout the listening men.

"You are here to fight! To battle against the enemies of peace! To wage unrelenting war against those alien forces of evil who threaten the welfare of our civilisation! I know that some of you may weaken. I know that some of you may be untrue to your glorious trust. To those I say, better death than dire shame. Be men, and live in glory. Be cowards, and fill a nameless grave."

He fell silent, his burning eyes roving the silent men. Gregg glanced at Merry, and caught a covert grin followed by a broad wink.

"Soon," the thin voice continued, "we shall enter hyper-space. There is a battle to be fought and won many light years from here. The enemy will be routed, but the struggle will not be easy. Time spent in training will not be wasted. That is all."

"Attention!" yelled the same furtive-eyed man. With a last proud glance at the lounging men, Alendi spun on his heel, and left the room.

Someone laughed. Next to Gregg, Merry exploded into action. One swift stride took him beside the grinning man. A great fist lifted, swung, and the man lay senseless.

"By God!" roared Merry, his eyes twin pools of flame. "I'll teach you dirt-grabbers to laugh at the Eagles." He stood over his victim, while from the clustered men came a low, animal-like growl.

Something gripped the ship and shook it. The tube lights faded, flickered; then burned bright again. A whine penetrated the vessel, shrilling higher and higher until it could no longer be heard. Breathing became difficult, mist seemed to fill the mess room, and slowly cleared.

They had entered hyper-space.

With the breaking from normal space into one in which faster than light travel was possible, anger left the men. The two groups, the shipmen, and the new recruits, looked at each other, the one contemptuous, the other fearful.

Merry laughed. "We're on our way," he yelled, "On to adventure, to battle, quick death and quick profits. The Warbirds are on the wing!"

Next to Gregg a man shoved forward, his face red from anger. Gregg recognised him for a new recruit, a hired hand from Lagos.

"What about our uniform?" he grumbled. "You said that we'd have cellosilk. This is like a sack."

A murmur came from the other recruits.

"Cellosilk?" Merry roared. "Who said that? I said you'd get free uniform, weapons, and ten credits a day. You're wearing your uniform. You'll be issued weapons when you need them. The pay you'll get when you've earned it."

"That's not fair," the man protested.

"Fair? Are you children to whine of fairness?" Merry sneered. "You'll wear cellosilk when you've earned it. When you've killed for it, not before." He swung to the gathered men. "Remember what you are. Warbirds. The scum of the universe. Unwanted, but necessary. You'll fight the aliens of a thousand worlds, and you'll fight the most deadly foe of all—men. Planets will employ you, pander to your very whim, and when the battles are over, kick you out. You'll do the dirty work of all the Galaxy—but you'll be paid for it, and paid well. Isn't that better than groveling in the dirt?"

His hand fell heavily on Gregg's shoulder.

"You all know this man. He joined with you. Will you trust him? Trust him to see that you get a fair deal?"

They looked hard, and they nodded. Gregg tried to protest, but the gripping hand on his shoulder kept him silent. Whatever game Merry was playing Gregg couldn't interfere. Later, in the cubicle they shared, Merry explained.

"On trips like this, first trips at any rate, I've found it pays to make a confidant of one of the new recruits. It allays the fears of others, and keeps things running smoothly."

"And after the first trip?" Gregg smiled. "I can imagine it would be awkward having too many confidantes.''

"If they don't die, or resign, I demote 'em." Merry flung himself on the bunk with a sigh of relief, and loosened his belt. "What did you think of Alendi?"

"I don't really know," said Gregg cautiously, remembering Merry's fury when the man had laughed.

"Don't worry about me beating you up," Merry said calmly. "I cracked down on that rookie for show. It helps discipline. Honestly now. What did you think of him?"

"I think I feel sorry for him," Gregg mused. "He must know the men ignore him, all that attention business, for example, but he paid no heed. I think he's a bit crazy."

"Yeah," Merry grunted. "Time was when he would have had the entire company standing stiff as pokers. Saluting, too. A great one for ceremonial was Alendi. Commander of a squadron of fifteen top-line ships. I was Captain of one of them." He spat thoughtfully.

"What happened?" Gregg was interested.

Merry shrugged. "The usual thing. We were hired to defend a system of five worlds. The enemy hired three times our number. Alendi wouldn't listen to reason. When it was all over, we had one ship, and our lives. Nothing else. He's never really recovered from the hyper-sonic. Still lives in the past. A good navigator, though, and he gets a fair amount of work."

"But all that nonsense about defenders of civilisation. Does he really believe all that?"

"Sure. Why not? If we didn't do the fighting for them, the worlds would re-arm." Merry squinted through a cloud of cigarette smoke. "Ever seen a world ruined by atomics? Or dusted, which is just as bad? I have." He shook his head. "It's a business. The way we fight no one gets hurt but us. The other way, whole planets go up in flame. Men, women, babies even, get slaughtered like cattle. It's all so senseless. Now they hire a group of Eagles and we fight for them. Beat the opposition and get paid off." He chuckled. "Wait until you see it. We set our own price."

"But if you lose?"

Merry shrugged. "We lose. The ship, cash, our lives even. Not always, though."

"How's that?"

"Surrender, and buy our way out."

Gregg nodded. He had heard of the Warbirds. Few hadn't. Misfits mostly. Men who sought in the rush and tide of battle, an outlet for violent emotion. Society condemned them, yet admired their necessity. Cultures shunned them—yet gladly used their services. Wars there were, and wars there would be, but technology had forced war to become a thing apart.

Nations, planets, dared not to fight. Gone were the days of indiscriminate killing. The dross from atomic piles was too plentiful, too deadly potent, for any state, no matter how powerful, to blast his neighbour. A single man, or woman, driven frantic with grief over the loss of a loved one, could load a ship with atomic dust, slip through the tightest cordon, and spread utter destruction.

Once spread, nothing could stop a world turning into an arid desert. Such planets were to be seen. Grown wealthy and arrogant, they had waged war, and died as a result.

And so the Warbirds. The Eagles. Mercenaries. Free Companions. Stateless men. Devoid of passion, hate and fear, they fought for money, and that alone. Men who could be trusted. Men who fought to a strict code. Battles were fought, and not a civilian died. Wars were lost, and not a city harmed. Losers paid, and paid dearly, but that was the total of their lives.

And he was one of them! Somehow Gregg didn't mind a bit.

The next few days were full of new experiences. Gun drill in the turrets. Aiming, loading, firing, rapping out coordinates, correcting errors, learning the delicate art of blasting a target into atoms.

Suit drill, wearing the clumsy space armour. Examining the outside of the ship, practising welding patches, getting used to the dim, grey ghostliness of hyper-space.

Merry took them in hand for close quarter combat. The sudden thrusts that caused nerve-tearing agony. The weak spots to be used in dealing death. Pistol practice, using moving targets, and electronic pistols. They hurt, but did not injure. After several severe shocks, even the dullest learned to keep low, and aim straight.

Gregg saw little of Owen. Sometimes he would catch a glimpse of the youth running errands, wearing a too-big uniform, and ludicrously carrying a holstered blaster. Sometimes, too, he would see the furtive-eyed, stooped little man, and when he saw them together hate shone clear in the little man's eyes.

He asked Merry about it.

"Who, Noxon?" Merry grinned. "Don't worry. He used to be Alendi's aide; now Owen's got his job. That means he'll have to fight." Merry rubbed fat hands together. "I've waited a long time to get my hands on that whining little runt. Now he's going to find out what it means to be an Eagle."

They were off duty, sprawling on the narrow bunks. Merry idly cleaned his pistol, whistling a mournful tune. Gregg put down the book on hyper-space navigation and bent across to Merry.

"Alendi said that we were off to fight. Who are we up against?"

Merry squinted down the gleaming barrel, and chuckled. "Eager for the fray, Gregg? Good. But it's only a routine job.

We get it every five years or so. Bread and butter work, but it will give the rookies experience, and pay for supplies."

"Where are we bound?"

"Prokeen. A Rim planet something like Lagos. There's a nest of vermin to clear out. Nasty, but not too dangerous. I don't reckon on many killed."

"Who did you say we're fighting?"

"I didn't." Merry chuckled again. "You'll find out in good time. How's the book work getting on?"

"O.K. I guess." Gregg glanced at the book. "I took this subject in school; wanted to be a pilot once."

"Why weren't you?"

"My folks needed help on the farm." He shrugged. "After they died, I couldn't get away; didn't really want to, and when I did, ships started missing Lagos altogether."

"A girl, Gregg?" Merry grinned lecherously.

"Perhaps."

Merry laughed. "Never mind. There's a hyper-radio station on Prokeen. You'll be able to call your girl. That is, if you can pay for the call."

"I'll be able to pay," said Gregg softly.

"How?"

Gregg smiled. "I've a friend named Merry. I'm sure he will oblige with a loan."

Merry looked at him strangely. "Maybe I will," he said slowly. "Maybe I will."

Outside the cubicle, someone screamed in mortal terror.

"Owen!" yelled Gregg, leaping for the door. Behind him Merry blundered, cursing. Owen cowered just beside the door, fumbling at the holstered gun. Noxon, eyes bloodshot, crouching like some unclean animal, weaved before him, a wicked looking knife gripped in a claw-like hand.

Before Gregg had taken in the scene, Merry had acted, thrusting Gregg to one side, he struck down with the newly cleaned pistol. The knife tinkled on the floor and Gregg kicked it aside. With one huge paw, Merry gripped the front of Noxon's uniform, and with surprising strength lifted him bodily.

"Scum!" he roared. "Want to fight, do you? Want to kill and threaten? Well, you'll get your chance." He jerked the limp form so that Noxon's head thudded against the metal bulkhead.

"Don't!" screamed the terror-stricken man. "I couldn't help it, Merry. I swear it. I meant 'im no 'arm. It was the drink that did it. The drink I tells yer."

Gregg caught a whiff of the man's breath. It carried a heavy, sickly-sweet odour. Even the little he smelt made his head spin. Merry seemed to go mad with fury.

"The drink did it, eh?" he mocked. With his free hand he slapped Noxon's face. A red welt appeared. "Blame the drink, will you?" Another slap. "Blame this on the drink then." Methodically he slapped the helpless man. Left, right. Left, right. The screaming died. The cursing faded. Noxon hung in Merry's grip like a broken doll. He dropped him to the floor.

"Where's the lad?"

Owen gave a choked answer.

"When you carry a gun, be ready to use it." Merry snatched the belted weapon from him. "What do you think this—a toy?"

"No, sir." Owen almost cried in his eagerness to please. "The Commander told me to carry it for him."

"He did, did he?" Merry growled. "Tell him I'll mind it for him. Here," he threw the weapon to Gregg, "keep this. Wear it under your shirt." He grew less irate.

"Remember, lad," he said to the still quivering Owen, "if you can't fight—run. Now what did you want?"

"Commander Alendi's compliments, sir. You are needed on the bridge."

"What does he want?" grumbled Merry. "I'm too busy to go running around for nothing."

Owen swallowed nervously. "I think it's to do with hyper-space." He looked appealingly at Gregg. "I heard him trying to contact the engine room. He said something about break-out in ten minutes."

Merry glanced at an instrument strapped to his thick wrist. "Blast!" he roared. "That engineer must be dead, or drunk." He turned to Owen. "Tell Alendi I'm attending to the trouble. Come on, Gregg." He ran down the passage towards the spiral staircase leading to the engine room.

"What's the trouble?" gasped Gregg, trying to keep up.

"Break-out time. If we don't break out of hyper-space on schedule, we'll be way off our destination. Have to hop around to get back. It'll mean wasted time, and maybe we'll lose the job." Merry reached the foot of the spiral, kicked open a door, and almost fell over a motionless figure.

"Drunk," he grunted after a hasty examination. "Wait until he can feel, I'll flay him inch by inch." Looking into the suddenly cruel features, Gregg wasn't at all sure he didn't mean it.

"What shall I do?" he asked.

"Get over to the controls. Can you operate them?"

"Yes," answered Gregg, after a quick examination. A large visi-screen stood over a control board. Like most war vessels, all essential controls were duplicated, so that it was possible to work the ship from the engine room alone.

"Good." Merry snapped on the intercom. "Merry to bridge. Engine room manned. Ready to break-out on signal."

A light flashed in response. "Commander to Engineer. Stand by for signal." Alendi's thin voice carried no surprise. Merry muttered and looked expressively at Gregg.

"Ready?"

Gregg nodded, hands on controls watching the screen. Nothing could be seen but the formless grey of hyper-space. An eternal medium where normal laws did not apply, and where speeds of fantastic nature did not confirm the speed mass-time formulae of Einstein. Only lucky discovery of hyper-flight had made the conquest of the Galaxy possible.

On the board before him lights flashed. Blue, amber, red. Gregg moved the controls. Behind him engines whined in sudden strained power. The ship shifted, slewed, spun, but paradoxically did not move. It was a movement of space rather than of the ship itself.

The engine room filled with fog, cleared, and on the screen, stars gleamed against darkness. They were through!

CHAPTER 3

PROKEEN

Prokeen, third planet of a giant red sun, was a world of stifling heat, rank vegetation, and thick, humid air. The people were dark-skinned, sultry-eyed, and apathetic. The climate had sapped the fierce colonising instincts of their forefathers, and they had drifted into easy-going listlessness.

Life was easy. The main export, perfume distilled from the riotous growth of exotic flowers, kept them in comparative wealth.

Merry looked at the colourful settlement and grunted contemptuously. "Shiftless lot. Maybe just as well, though, it gives us work of a sort." He spat in the thick dust of the landing field.

"When do we start?" Gregg sniffed appreciatively at the scented air.

"Soon. Alendi's discussing terms now. A formality, of course. We're in no position to argue. Any group would be glad of the job."

"What is this mysterious job?"

Merry chuckled. "An extermination project. Simple." He laughed at the bewildered look on Gregg's face. "The original natives of this planet breed at a regular rate of increase. When the population exceeds a certain figure they move. They are due to move on the settlement, and we are here to kill off the surplus."

"But why don't the people themselves attend to it? Negotiate a treaty or something?"

"The Dreeda aren't human, Gregg. A cross between spiders, and the devil himself. Not human, but not unintelligent either. Our job is to wipe them out in the immediate vicinity of the settlement." He looked up at the rocket.

"Still busy. I know Alendi and his eternal love of ceremony. Let's find a wine shop."

Gregg nodded and followed Merry into the town. He looked with interest at the dark-skinned people. They looked at him with equal interest. A young girl, long black hair threaded with giant blooms, caught at his arm and smiled up at him.

"Hello, Warbird. You stay here long?"

Her voice was low, husky, and caressing. Merry, looking back over one shoulder, grinned. "Time for love later, sweetheart. See him after the Dreeda are dead."

She slipped from Gregg's arms, smiling invitation and promise, and mingled with the crowd. A singer, lying inelegantly in the dust, caroled a lilting song, playing some weird stringed instrument. Naked children raced between the legs of the elders, laughter following them like a cloud.

Merry disappeared into a low doorway, vine-wreathed and cool looking. Gregg followed and joined him at a table. A smiling woman served them with thick, ruby wine, refusing the coins Merry offered as payment. He grinned after her.

"Nice people, Gregg." He slowly rotated the blown glass goblet, watching the turgid motion of the wine. "It wouldn't be too hard to settle down here. Pretty women, easy climate, plenty for all." He watched Gregg over the brim of the glass.

"Not for me. A little of it would be nice, too much would sicken. I want to see the stars, roam the worlds. Enjoy all the different aspects of life, not just a local paradise." Gregg felt a little drunk, the wine coursed hotly through his blood, unused to any but the crude distillations of Lagos.

Merry grinned, and reached for the jug. His hand stopped in mid-air. From the sun-drenched street noise burst like a rattle of gunfire. Shouts, screams, glass smashing. The wine-shop woman dashed past them, her face ugly with strain and panic.

"The Dreeda! The Dreeda!" Sheer horror rang in every word.

Gregg reached the street in a single bound, and stood blinking in the bright glare, tugging at his hidden blaster. Something scuttled along the road, and suddenly he felt very sick. Behind him he heard Merry's deep curse, and the roar of a weapon. Flame lanced from behind him, so close that he could feel the heat scorch his flesh, then the blaster came free and he began shooting at everything in sight.

He couldn't miss. The street was full of them. About five feet high. Six-legged, ant-like in their armour and mandibles, yet with writhing tentacles sprouting from four-eyed heads, grasping futilely at barred windows and locked doors.

The Dreeda! Underworld spawn of this planet, broken out of their tunnels, seeking the warm-bloodied prey on which they doted. The pile of shattered bodies mounted before him. Then Merry was shouting in his ear, and the red tide of battle slowly cleared away.

"Let up, Gregg. They're all dead."

Shaking his head, he gingerly approached the still twitch-ing heap of seared bodies. Legs, delicate in their ebon armour, kicked in reflex action. Great saw-edged mandibles clashed in dying ferocity. From the corpses oozed a thin green ichor, and a fetid odour poisoned the air.

Gregg wiped his streaming brow and for the first time no-ticed the long, ugly scratch running across his torso through a shirt as if with a razor. He smiled weakly and gladly drained the pot the woman fetched from the wine shop.

"Near squeak, Merry. So they're the Dreeda. Seem easy meat to me."

Merry shook his head. "Don't get careless, Gregg. They are nocturnal. The sun slowed them down, almost blinded them. Meet them in their own tunnels and you'll find them far from easy."

He reached for the jug and drained it in one giant swallow. "I'd better report to Alendi. We had better start at once. You stay here, and keep your weapon ready; there may be more, but I doubt it." He kicked at the heap of broken flesh. "Probably an isolated raiding party. Must be pretty desperate to try it in daylight."

He grinned. "Not scared, are you?"

"No. But hurry it up, will you? I want another crack at them. I'm no nursemaid."

"You'll give them morale." Merry jerked his head at the timidly approaching group of colonists. "Better get that scratch attended to, may be poisoned; the woman will give you some salve." He winked. "Maybe more than just salve, too."

Gregg cursed him good-naturedly as he swung away. The wound had begun to throb and burn, and he gladly accepted the sticky ointment the woman eagerly brought him, He felt uncomfortable; the naked adoration in her eyes was hard to ignore. It was hero worship, he knew, but he was still young enough to be impressed.

"You are brave," she said, resting one hand lightly on his arm.

"Nothing to it. I had a blaster." He tried to sound offhanded about the whole thing. "What were they after?"

She shuddered, and moved closer. "Men, women, children, anything warm-blooded. Their young thrive when hatched on meat." She smiled carelessly. "Never mind now. We are safe with you brave Warbirds to protect us. You will kill them all, and then," she smiled more warmly, "perhaps you will stay with us? You would be so very welcome."

Gregg desperately tried to change the subject. "Do you run the wine shop alone? Where is your husband?"

"Dead," she sighed. "He was careless and went too far into the jungle alone." She dabbed at her eyes. "It is hot out here. Will you sit in the cool? It will aid your wound, for you must be careful, the Dreeda are sometimes poisonous."

She gently drew him into the dark coolness of the tavern.

* * * *

The opening yawned raw and moist in the depths of the jungle. The edges of the crater had fallen, but the hole could still be seen, dark and threatening with promise of unknown terrors far from the light of the sun.

Gregg shifted uneasily in his armour, and cursed the heat. He wished that he could remove the helmet. His nose itched, and the scratch still burned. He eased the broad straps of his equipment, settling the weight of blasters, machete, and charges more evenly. On his back the pack of rations, and the cylinders of a portable flame caster ground in delicate flesh. He snarled in temper at the grinning Merry.

"When the hell do we get out of this heat?"

"In a hurry to get back to the wine shop?" Merry sniggered. "If I hadn't arrived when I did, we'd have lost a Warbird and gained an innkeeper." He laughed suggestively, the other dozen men joining in.

Gregg ground his teeth, then laughed with the rest. "O.K., but I'll be drinking free when you are buying your wine. How much longer, Merry?"

"Not long. We must wait until the other parties have sealed the tunnels and are ready to attack at the same time." He looked suddenly serious. "Now, listen, and I'm not talking just to make a noise. When you get into the tunnels, it'll be fight, fight all the way. Shoot first, quick and often, but remember that you've only a certain amount of charges, when they are gone the Dreeda must be dead, or we will."

"How long will this engagement take, Captain?" A rookie asked the question, and Noxon snarled at him, "'Ow do we know? It took two weeks last time."

"Shut up, Noxon. It depends on how many there are; how well we fight; and what luck we have. I guess about ten days, but it could be less."

The portable radio Merry carried bleeped, and he lifted a hand for silence. Squeaky noises came from the earpiece and he made terse answers. "Tunnels sealed? Good." He glanced at his wrist. "Five minutes? Are you certain? I think so. No, Alendi. Don't be crazy, man, it's murder." He looked at Gregg. "I know all about that, but use your head, what good is a dead man?" He listened again, and snorted in sheer contempt. "As you wish," he finished coldly. "But you'll answer for it." He broke the connection.

"Alendi's decided that Owen should get experience in the tunnels," he said, not looking at Gregg.

"But he can't!" Gregg leapt to his feet. "The man's mad. Owen's just a kid, he's never even fired a gun in his life." He appealed to Merry. "Stop it somehow. Owen's no Warbird. He only joined up because I did. What possible use could he be?"

"None." Merry looked sour. "But Alendi thinks otherwise. Treat 'em rough, and may the best survive. I'm sorry, Gregg, but there's nothing you can do about it now." He looked at his wrist again. "We attack in two minutes."

"That be damned." Gregg jumped up again. "Where are they? I'm going to stop it."

"Sit down!" Merry grated the command in a tone Gregg had never heard use. The blaster in his hand pointed directly at him, rock-steady in the gloved fist. Gregg felt a peculiar feeling in the pit of the stomach, but he made no move to sit.

"If you don't sit down, I'll blast your legs from under you."

"What's come over you, Merry?"

"Nothing. While we're at it, remember something else. I'm Captain Merry to you, and to all you other scum. Captain Merry, and don't you forget it!"

"Are you crazy?"

"Try moving away and find out. I mean it, Harmond. Take a step and I'll kill you." Something in the narrowed eyes warned Gregg that he wasn't making an idle threat. Boiling with rage, he slumped down on the edge of the hole.

The others made no effort to hide their grins. Gregg was unpopular. Close association with Merry had gained him the undeserved reputation of being favoured, and they gloried in his discomfiture. Merry glanced at his wrist.

"Ready. On your feet. Follow me." He leapt into the crater, Gregg close behind.

It was pitch dark in the tunnel. The narrow opening widened to a smooth passageway about ten feet across, and in the light of their flash lamps, the sides showed the unmistakable signs of the Dreeda. Their horny bodies had cut shallow grooves, and their serrated jaws had carved an eerie fresco in the close packed soil.

Merry led the way, his lamp throwing a brilliant wash of light ahead of them. Beside him two men crouched, guns at the ready. Gregg, with the flame-thrower, brought up the rear. They made no sound, but following the huge bulk of the captain advanced almost at a run. Behind them the tiny spot of light that marked the exit dwindled to a dot, then vanished.

For over a mile, they met nothing, then something scuttled with frightful speed towards them, a gun roared, and they climbed over a twitching body. A few yards further on the tunnel divided, and Merry stopped, gathering the men around him.

"From now on the going gets tough. That back there was a sentry; we'll meet a few old ones for a while, but as we get nearer to the centre, they'll attack in force. Now, remember, the object is to get to the breeding cells. The Dreeda are sterile. Kill the queen, and the new hatched brood, and we'll clear the area for about five years."

"What about the grown ones?" The question came tremblingly from the lips of one of the men. Merry flashed him a quick glance of scorn. "Kill 'em on the way out."

He glanced at the dividing passage.

"We'll have to seal that. Can't have them attacking from the rear. Noxon. Take a bomb and set it about five hundred yards down. Gregg. Take three men and cover him. Get back here as soon as you can. Quick now."

Gingerly taking the pre-set bomb, the little man waited for his escort and headed down the passage. Counting his steps, Gregg stopped when he thought they had traveled far enough, and gestured to Noxon.

Hastily settling the cylinder against one wall, he pressed a stud, and without waiting for the others, raced back down the passage. Gregg, lingering to see that the others were clear, spun on his heel and followed them.

He could see the bobbing lights ahead, the dim shapes silhouetted against them throwing giant shadows onto the walls of the passage. Fear speeded his feet. Imagination sent prickles running along his spine. Almost he could feel the horrible jaws gaping behind him.

Thankfully he stumbled into the other passage, and raced towards where Merry and the others sprawled flat. As he reached them, a giant hand picked him up and threw him forward. A roaring explosion almost cracked his eardrums, and he rolled over clawing his way out of dirt. Through the echoes he heard a man's panicky scream: "My Gawd. We've blown the roof in. We can't get out!"

As the dust settled Gregg could see what he meant. Behind them, along the route to safety, the entire roof had collapsed. They were trapped!

CHAPTER 4

THE DREEDA

Merry flicked the switch of the radio, then flung the entire instrument down in disgust. "Broken!"

Noxon began whining, and Merry turned on him in sudden fury. "Shut up! You're not dead yet." He turned to the others. "We'll get to the breeding cells. Meet up with the other parties, and use their escape route." He pursed his lips. "The bomb must have had too heavy a charge. Better be careful of using the rest."

"What do we do now, Captain?" Gregg barely troubled to conceal his sarcasm.

"Do? Why, go on, of course." He look sharply at Gregg. "Better keep that flame-thrower ready, Harmond. Stay at the rear. When I yell, use it." He stood, head bent in a listening attitude. "Line up, men. I think they're coming."

Gregg squinted down the tunnel. Hastily the men took up their positions, throwing their massed lights forward. In the brilliant light, what seemed to be a black river flowed. It raced nearer, slowed as the lights hit it, then came on again, pushed by forces behind. It wasn't a river.

As he watched the incredibly rapid advance, Gregg understood Merry's warning. They ran with almost the speed of horses, bounding along on all six legs, jaws clashing before them, tentacles lashing the air in all directions. A moment he had for study, then the men blazed into action.

Fire spouted from a dozen weapons. Black ebon armour crisped in the heat; bodies crashed lifeless to the floor, but even though dead, those bodies kept advancing, pressed forward by the hordes behind. Closer came the pile of dead, piling higher and higher under the flaming fury of the Warbirds' guns.

The air grew thick with a greasy black smoke. Thin rivulets of green ichor puddled the floor, and still the insane ferocity of the attack continued. The press was too great, the men, frantically firing as they were, just couldn't kill fast enough to stop it.

Merry, a roaring blaster in each hand, stepped back out of the front line. Gregg saw his face beneath the smoke-blackened visor of his helmet. Saw, but could not hear, the shouted command. With a gloating feeling he lifted the heavy nozzle of the flame thrower. At last he could come into action.

He sent the first short blast high above the head of the men before him. As one man they dropped to the floor. The Dreeda, unopposed, surged forward, tentacles clutching at the men helpless before them. Gregg, a tight hard smile on his lips, triggered the heavy weapon.

A finger of intense brilliance stabbed from the nozzle. Even through the smoked glass of his visor his eyes smarted and began to water. Like a hose he played the flame on the writhing mass before him, and where the flame rested, life ceased.

Heat! Heat generated by the liberation of atomically unstable elements. Heat so great that the very temperature of the air began to rise at an alarming rate. It was an emergency weapon. One that could only be used for a short period, and for a strictly limited time. A dangerous weapon. One that could only be used at great risk of an explosion that would wipe out the user and everything in the immediate vicinity, but it was a weapon that worked!

The flame died. Where a hideously surging tide of insect-like bodies had blackened the tunnel, ash, dust, and a few

seared and broken remnants lay. From the charred heap fig-
ures stirred, and painfully scorched men climbed to their feet.

Not all of them. Merry leaned down, pulled at a limp
shape, and grunted. Gregg caught a glimpse of a face that
even in death still bore a look of horror, and felt suddenly
sick. They had had their first casualty.

"Good work, Gregg," Merry grunted, stripping the dead
body of food and weapons. "For a while I thought they'd
got us. Never known them so desperate before." He stood up
wincing. "Noxon!"

"Yeah?"

"Carry this stuff. The rest of you O.K.? Then get a move
on. We've a long way to go."

The little group moved on into the black terror of the tunnel. Behind, a solitary figure kept eyeless vigil.

* * * *

By the fifth day, Gregg knew that they were hopeless-
ly lost. All the tunnels were the same, the radio, on which
they had relied to keep contact with the other groups, and by
which they could have got their bearings, had long since been
discarded.

They plunged on, a diminished group now, in a blind hope
to find the breeding cells and a chance of meeting the others.

It had become routine. They snatched sleep where and
when they could, one half of them always keeping guard.
They drank sparingly at the water in their canteens, munched
tediously on tasteless vitamin concentrates.

Gregg thought of Owen somewhere in this maze, and
cursed in blind, impotent fury. He thought of the men they
had lost. Of Nichols, screaming as cruel jaws pinched him in
half. Of Samuels, begging for a quick death after poisoned
claws had ripped the helmet from his head, and torn his face

to tatters. Of the two others, carried off to some unknown fate, while they watched helpless to even end their pain.

He grew callous, brutal almost, in his disregard of suffering. His own body ached and burned. Death ceased to have any meaning, and hope was a lost dream. Owen, however was different.

Merry, a blackened, giant figure, whipping them on by sheer will-power, paused at a branching passageway. He looked closely at the floor, studied the sides, even slid back his faceplate, and gingerly sniffed the air. When he looked up he was grinning.

"At last! I think that this is what we've been looking for. See the scraping on the sides? The downward slope of the tunnel? I'll bet my hope of a jug of wine against a spent charge, that it leads to the breeding cells. Come on."

"Wait!" snapped Gregg curtly. "If it does lead to the cells, it'll be well guarded. Better check equipment; and how about sealing the tunnel behind us?"

Merry nodded thoughtfully. "It's worth the chance. We can't be any worse off. Set the bombs then, Gregg. I'll set them off by remote control." He chuckled. "We don't want the roof coming down on top of us."

The bombs set, they advanced down. When they had covered a good half-mile, Merry spun a small handle on a compact box. Behind them, the very soil churned in the throes of the twin explosions.

Noxon whimpered, and Merry cursed him foully. "Blast you for a yellow cur, Noxon! You've grown soft as Alendi's aide. Now you'll earn your keep. Gregg. Give him the flame-thrower."

"No! I don't want it. I won't take it, I tells yer." The man was livid with fright.

"Why not?" Merry grinned cruelly. "You'll be in the rear, nothing to do but turn on the heat when I signal." He glared into the other's face. "Take it, and if you turn yellow, I'll blast you down if it's my last act."

Gregg thankfully passed over the weapon. The charge was getting low, the nozzle pitted, and the danger of a flash-back highly possible. Noxon strapped it to his back, uttering silent curses.

Once again the small group plunged into the winding tunnels. They met little opposition, and Merry grew worried. "It's not natural," he confided to Gregg. "We should have met them before this if we are heading right. I don't like it."

"Maybe they're waiting for us further down?" Greg suggested. "Saving their forces to wipe us out, perhaps."

Merry shook his head. "That's not the way they fight, Gregg. They operate on pure instinct when it comes to defending the cells. No. There's another reason."

They found it a mile down the tunnel.

It was plain to see what had happened. The crisped bodies. The widening of the tunnel, the walls glistening in the lights, telling of the intense heat that had fused them. A flame-thrower had exploded. Of its operator, of the rest of the group, there was no trace, unless a little heap of ash could be called traces.

Gregg stood for a long moment looking down at them. Was Owen there? he wondered. He had no time for idle speculation, Merry was running down the passage urgently waving them after him. "Quick! To the cells before they have time to send up more fighters," he gasped, with the titanic effort of forcing his huge body along.

"We had luck back there. They took the charge, and wiped them out. Pity their flame-thrower exploded, though, we could have combined forces.

"Luck you call it?" Gregg sounded bitter.

Merry shrugged. "Rather them than us." He stopped, pointing down the tunnel. "Look!" There was exultation in his voice. "The cells! At last we've found the cells!"

Dim and ghostly in the distance, a pale light gleamed with the blue-green of decay. They had arrived at last!

The breeding cells of the Dreeda were in a vast cavern hollowed out of the depths of the planet. Tunnels radiated from it. From the mass of rotting flesh, decomposed vegetation, and fetid slime on the floor, a pale, wavering light shone. Squatting in the centre of the cavern was the Queen. The huge body was bloated beyond all resemblance to the hideous, but alienly graceful Dreeda. The spiderly legs were useless; the great jaws atrophied; from the distended abdomen dripped a continual stream of waxy eggs. Attendants caught them, ran into the tunnels, or gently placed them in far corners of the huge cavern. Over the entire expanse of the floor, tiny new-hatched Dreeda wallowed, their jaws working incessantly as they ate the mess.

To Gregg, crouching just within one of the tunnels, the scene was one of utter horror.

Merry chuckled grimly. "This is luck. Before they can bring up fresh guards we'll have cleared the chamber." He gestured to the men.

"Listen. The first thing is to get the queen, then the Dreeda, lastly we'll sterilize the chamber. Noxon! Stand by with the flame-thrower. When we need it, we're going to need it quick. Ready?"

They grunted, hands gripped tight around the butts of weapons. Nerves hardened against the ordeal to come.

"Come. Let's go." Merry stepped within the cavern and sent a livid blast towards the squatting obscenity of the queen. It struck full on the nightmare head, and the gross bulk quivered. Strangely it screamed.

Gregg had never before heard any of the Dreeda utter a sound. The high-pitched inhuman shriek sounded as loud as a ship's siren. It stunned him for a second with its utter unexpectedness. As if moved by one common brain all the Dreeda within the cavern stopped, spun to face them, and in a solid black mass charged in an irresistible tide towards them.

It was impossible to halt the charge. Merry yelled to Noxon, signalling frantically with his arm and dropping to the floor. The others followed, still firing futilely at the advancing horde. It was useless. Nothing but the terrible power of the flame-thrower could halt them.

Noxon stood as paralysed, the heavy nozzle sagging in his hands. Torn between the dread of using the weapon, and the certainty of death if he didn't, his nerve snapped, and with a wild scream he turned and raced back up the passage down which they had come.

Gregg, turning to see why he hadn't got the weapon in action, saw the fleeing figure. For a moment, shocked unbelief numbed him. Without the flame-thrower they were all as good as dead. Noxon, too, for there was no escape the way he was running.

Leaping to his feet, Gregg chased after him. "Noxon," he yelled, "Come back, you fool!"

The first shot missed; the second knocked the running man's legs from beneath him. In seconds he had reached the writhing shape, torn the weapon from his back, and stumbling with haste rejoined his comrades.

He was barely in time. Even as he raised the nozzle, a man, shrieking in terror, was lifted from the tiny group, flung into the air and caught between snapping jaws. Then the lance of flame spouted, and like a man with a hose washing the street, he washed the cavern clean.

Steadily he advanced. Before him the glistening black hordes vanished into puffs of ash. The nozzle grew hot within his hands, a hissing came from the weapon, and suddenly someone was tugging at his arm, yelling in desperate fury.

"Get rid of it, Gregg. Get rid of it, quick!"

With sudden panic, he flung the weapon away from him, and obeying instinct, dropped to the floor. Sound tore at him; something thudded into his helmet. Heat from the very gates of hell washed over him, searing skin and singeing hair.

Half stunned, he lifted his head and gazed stupidly around. The cavern was clean, not even the newly-hatched moved amid the now crisp rubbish on the floor. Something warm ran down the side of his face, and near him a man laughed in hysterical relief.

Merry clapped him on the shoulder, and stared anxiously in his helmet. "God, man, but you're lucky. If you'd had the thrower strapped on..." He shrugged. "You didn't, and you saved us all." Anger darkened his blackened features. "Where's that yellow dog, Noxon?"

Gregg gestured weakly towards the tunnel. "I had to shoot him. I think he's dead."

"Go and make sure," Merry ordered one of the men. "If he isn't, kill him." He grinned at Gregg. "Well, we did it. All we have to do now is to find a way out."

Next to him a man yelled warning, lifting a blaster in a leaden hand. From one of the tunnels something entered the cavern. Lights flashed from them, and they walked on two legs. Merry knocked the blaster and laughed with relief. "Don't shook. It's one of the other parties." And then without even troubling to lower his voice, "Alendi, and late as usual."

Gregg stared at the party, searching for Owen. The helmets hid their faces, but as he peered a sick feeling gripped him. He stopped before the tall figure of the Commander.

"Where's Owen?"

"Owen? Ah, yes, my aide." Alendi shrugged carelessly. "Gone, I fear. He was very stupid. It's little loss, he would never have made a Warbird."

"Gone! Dead, do you mean?"

One of the other men stepped forward. "He got it at the first engagement. Never even fired a gun." He dropped a sympathetic hand on Gregg's shoulder. "It was quick. He didn't even scream."

Gregg shook off the restraining hand. "You murderer!" he snarled at the tall Commander. "You knew that he couldn't last five minutes in this hell, and you forced him to go with you. Why did you do it?"

Alendi shrugged. "It is not for you to question me, a Commander of a Group. The boy proved himself unfit. He is better gone. Now no more on this matter. Captain, gather your men. We will return." He swung on his heel and moved towards the tunnel.

Gregg took a step after him, one hand reaching for the weapon at his side. Merry gripped him, spun him around with surprising force, and glared into the helmet. "Not now, Gregg!" he hissed. "I know how you feel, but not now. Understand?"

He nodded dumbly, and suddenly darkness overwhelmed him. He remembered nothing of the return journey to the surface.

CHAPTER 5

VICTORY

Merry was very drunk. He sprawled in the vine-wreathed wine-shop and morosely downed great quantities of the thick ruby wine. In the town the people celebrated the extermination of their enemy, the Dreeda. He watched them with little eyes hot with anger.

He looked up a commotion at the door, and waved his pot in greeting. "Here, Gregg. Did you make your call?"

Gregg nodded absently. He looked older, thinner. A faint scar creased his left temple, and his eyes held a hard, cynical look, only recently acquired. He slumped into a vacant chair and accepted the jug Merry thrust at him.

"Thanks."

"Make contact without trouble?" Merry was curious.

"Yeah." Gregg fell silent, feeling again the pain of his recent hyperbeam radio call. Jean had seemed glad to see him, eager for news they had talked for a while, then, as he had dreaded, she had asked for news of her brother.

He had told her as gently as possible.

"Dead?" She seemed unable to believe it. "You mean that I'll never see him again?"

"I'm afraid so, Jean."

"How did it happen?" Her voice sounded dull and listless. He told her, emphasising the painlessness of Owen's death, adding to the glory of it. Even to him to sounded false.

"I see," she nodded. "He followed you, fool that he was, and now he's dead."

"That's not fair, Jean," he had protested. "I had nothing to do with it. I didn't even know he had joined until we were in space."

"If you hadn't joined then, he would still be alive." Tears brimmed her eyes. "It's just as father said. If you had done your duty to the community, instead of running off at the first bit of hardship, Owen would be here now."

"But—"

"It doesn't matter. I never want to see or hear from you again, Gregg Harmond. Do you understand?" Without waiting for an answer she had broken the connection.

Gregg swallowed deeply at the contents of his jug. "Yeah, I made contact—for the last time, too."

Merry grunted sympathetically. "Breaking old ties is hard, I know." He glowered into the wine. "I've been with Alendi for a long time. I'm beginning to think that it's been too long."

"What are you driving at?"

"This." Merry waved outside. "I never wanted to become a pest exterminator. Burrowing in the dirt like animals. Twenty dead men, and enough charges used to fight a war, and what do we get for it? Bare pay, that's what."

Gregg shrugged. "It's work. What are you whining about? You can resign, can't you?"

"Why should I? The ship is as much mine as Alendi's. I've recruited for him, knocked the crews into shape, done all the dirty work, and still he treats me like dirt. You know where he is now?" He breathed wine into Gregg's face.

"Where?"

"With the Directors of the settlement. Talking like a fool about the glory of dying. Talking himself right out of a bonus, more likely. I've seen it happen before."

"What of it?"

"Is that what you want, Gregg? I remember a time when you almost killed Alendi. If I hadn't stopped you, you'd be dead meat by now. Have you forgotten Owen?"

"Leave Owen out of it."

"Can we? But leave him out it. There's quick wealth waiting for a man with guts and brains, Gregg. I know all the dodges, the short cuts, the easy ways. Follow Alendi and wind up in a rat-hole like Owen did. Do as I say, and we'll have an empire." Merry sucked in his lips, and for a moment naked lust for power shone from his narrowed eyes.

Gregg sat musing, slowly turning the wine jug between his palms. Merry was right! Wealth could do anything. Could even make a girl on some distant planet change her views about him. After all, wasn't that the reason he had joined the Warbirds? Why be squeamish?

"What's your suggestion?" he asked casually.

Merry leaned forward eagerly. "I'm expecting an old friend. He radioed me that his ship is due in tonight." He chuckled. "Too late, of course, for the job they had in mind, but we can always work something out. We'll join forces. Depose the Commanders, and strike out afresh."

"How are you going to depose the Commanders? And who is going to be the new one? You?"

Surprisingly, Merry shook his head. "No. I'm too well known. We need a new man, someone with brains, guts, and drive." He grinned. "I know just the man."

Gregg drank his wine.

* * * *

Fenson was a villainous-looking man. An old injury had scarred his face, but he was surprisingly well educated, even though sometimes careless in his talk. He greeted Merry with a yell, and they settled down to discussing old times. Listening to their talk, Gregg could imagine the wide-flung places of the Galaxy, the fabled Centre from which flowed wealth and power. He heard talk of empires, of daring adventurers who had climbed the thrones of kings. Mercenaries, who after a few years of blazing action, had settled down to a life of ease.

They spoke familiarly of exotic haunts, mysterious worlds of mind-tingling pleasure; strange aliens, and stranger drugs. Between them, across a wine-stained table, old wars were fought, mighty empires laid low; the gossip of a whole universe idly chatted over a jug of wine.

Gregg felt his blood warm as the tales were told. It seemed that there was little that a strong man of action could not do. Suddenly, he felt dis-satisfied with the narrow circle of existence as he had known it. The softer pleasures of nature had never appealed to him. Now, hardened by the recent action, he felt eager for fresh conquests.

Merry winked at Fenson, and turned to Gregg. "Sorry to ignore you, Gregg, but my old friend and I had a lot to talk over. He's with Maxwell's Invincibles." He laughed. "And about as broke as we are."

"Let's cut out the subterfuge," Gregg snapped. "I'm not dumb. You said something a while ago. Did you mean it?"

Fenson glanced sharply at Merry, raising his eyebrows. Merry nodded reassuringly. "Gregg's O.K. Everything settled at your end?"

Fenson nodded slowly. "Yes. Who is going to lead the Group? I can't, neither can you. I don't trust any of my men, and I don't think much of yours."

Merry grinned. "We took on fresh recruits a while back. Gregg is one of them. I tried him out, and he's got guts, education too. He doesn't love Alendi, and he's an unknown. Suit you?"

"Wait a minute," Gregg snapped. "I've got something to say about this. Why can't either of you take over the Group? Why an unknown? Why me?"

"Are you scared?" sneered Merry. "We can't because the Arsenals have blacklisted us. We want an unknown because your methods will be new; your reputation whatever we choose to make it. What's the matter, Gregg? Don't you want to become the Commander of a double Group?"

Gregg nodded. "Why not? But listen, you two, and get this straight! Advice is one thing, but I'm no puppet to be used as you think fit. If I'm Commander, then I'll be Commander. No split command, no two bosses; you'll do as I say, and like it! Agreed?"

Fenson shoved back his chair. "Not so fast, Harmond. If you think we're going to drop this right in your lap for the fun of it, think again."

Merry grabbed his arm. "Wait. We wanted someone with guts, didn't we? Well, here he is. We'll get our cut, and we'll do as he says. If he flops on the job, we'll get rid of him. If not, then we'll be with him all the way. Agreed?"

Gregg scooped the wine jug off the table. "I promise you that I'll lead the Group to wealth, action, and maybe sudden death." He grinned. "One thing only can I be certain of—I'll not let you down. Will you drink to that?"

When the jug returned to the table it was empty.

* * * *

Merry explained on their way back to the ship. "Fenson and I have had this planned for a long time. Maxwell is like Alendi, getting old and scared. Taking on the little jobs, the dirty work. Both of them are past their prime." He drew in a deep breath. "Tomorrow we'll be away, a new Group, and to hell with all this mucking about in the dirt for a living."

"How are we going to depose Alendi and Maxwell?"

"Fenson will take care of Maxwell. I'll handle Alendi. You'll have to register with the Arsenal, though."

"What is the Arsenal?" Gregg was curious. "I've heard you mention it before."

Merry grinned. "The only thing which stops us being hunted down as pirates is the fact that we're registered with the Arsenal. You wouldn't know much about it living on the Rim, but in the centre a whole system of worlds gets a profitable living by the manufacture and sale of arms and ships. We call them the Arsenal. You'll have to report every movement, every engagement, every new recruit to them."

"And if we don't?"

"You must, Gregg. Obviously, we can't carry a ton or two of gold about with us. The Arsenal acts as InterGalactic bankers; they keep our credit, supply us with ammunition, keep us informed of any work going. Without them we'd just be scavengers. If we don't register we'll be shot down on sight by any patrol ship, or Group for that matter."

"What's the procedure?"

"You'll report Maxwell's and Alendi's abdication—if you can call it that. Register your name, the official documents from the local Director affirming the change. Then you'll be credited with whatever is in the kitty, and we're on our own."

Merry clapped a hand on Gregg's shoulder.

"Don't worry about it. I'll steer you through."

They had arrived at the ship. Gregg stared curiously at the new arrival. If anything, it looked even more battered than his own. Merry called down to him, and he ran lightly up the ramp.

Alendi was alone in his cabin when they arrived. The ship was as very quiet. Most of the men were enjoying themselves in the town. From the sick bay came a low moaning from some injured man; other than that, nothing disturbed the silence.

Merry was very curt. "Alendi. I've come to tell you that you are deposed. What are you going to do about it?"

For a moment the tall, thin Commander stared at them in amazement, then as the import of Merry's words registered, anger took hold of him. "Are you mad?" The thin voice held biting contempt. "You tell me that I am deposed? You?" The eyes burned in the paper-white face, the thin lips writhed. "Get out!"

Merry stood his ground. "I mean it, Alendi. Like it or not, you're finished. Forget your crazy pride for a while. What do you intend doing about it?"

"Do?" One slender hand moved in a lightning gesture. Suddenly it held a blaster. "Get out. Report to the brig. I'll conduct your court martial in the morning. Now move!"

Merry sighed and glanced at Gregg. "Listen, Alendi. Can't you understand? The crew have deposed you. You're out. Shooting me won't make any difference."

"I said, get out."

Watching him, Gregg felt a quiver of fear. The man was as perfectly capable of shooting them both, and would consider himself justified in doing so. Merry doggedly stood his ground, his own anger swelling his thick neck.

"Listen, Alendi. I've been with you a long time, and I'm telling you that this is the end. I won't ship with a madman, and neither will the crew. Not one of them has signed on. You haven't even got an aide, let along enough men to work the ship. You're beaten, Alendi. Do you understand? You're finished. Washed up. A failure."

For a moment Gregg thought he would fire. The thin hand tightened on the weapon, knuckles whitened with strain, then he slumped. All the stiffness seemed to leave him. The fierce pride alone allowed him to stand erect. Watching him wilt was like watching a man slowly die.

Merry quietly left the cabin. Once outside, Gregg started to speak, but Merry checked him with a sharp gesture. He waited until they were some distance away, then blew a sign of relief. "That was close. I thought the old devil would burn us both."

"What now?"

"Nothing. We just wait." Merry looked at the bridge.

Gregg nodded, entered the radio room, and snapped switches. Fenson's face appeared on the visi-screen. He grinned as he saw Gregg.

"Hello, Commander. Maxwell has just had a fatal seizure. He was an old man. Is Merry there?"

A roar echoed throughout the ship. Something fell heavily to the floor. From the sick bay, a man yelled weak questions. Merry came through the door wiping his face. He looked very pale.

"Hello, Fenson," he called to the screen. "Alendi's just shot himself. Couldn't take being deposed, I guess. How's Maxwell?"

"Dead."

The two Captains grinned at each other via the screen.

Gregg felt suddenly sick.

CHAPTER 6

THE ARSENAL

Even by hyperbeam it took a long time to contact the Arsenal. Gregg waited numbly before the screen as it swirled with shifting changes of colour, and mentally rehearsed his story. The Directors of the settlement had willingly attested to the natural deaths of the two Commanders. Gregg suspected that judicious bribes combined with subtle threats had helped him to sign the papers. They had them, however, and murder or not, they were safe.

The screen cleared and a clerical-looking man stared at him. "Arsenal here. Registration section."

Gregg bent to the screens. "Harmond calling. Late of Alendi's Undefeateds. I wish to register the deaths of Commanders Maxwell and Alendi."

"One moment. Please show official registration of deaths. Give Galactic co-ordinates. Stand by."

Gregg rapped out the co-ordinates, and pressed the official documents to the screen. He knew that they were being photographed, and the signatures and thumb prints compared with those in the official files. When the screen again cleared the man was smiling pleasantly.

"All seems to be in order. What can we do for you?"

"I want to disband the two Groups and recombine them under new title. All assets to be fused and rendered available."

"Certainly. I'll check your credits. What name do you wish to register under? Who is the Commander? Who are your Captains?"

"Commander Harmond, Gregg Harmond."

"Yes, and the name?"

Gregg frowned, he hadn't thought of a name.

He remembered Alendi and the man's fierce pride. What had he called them?

"Tell me. Is the name Eagles registered?"

"Eagles?" The man looked surprised. "Oh, I remember. An extinct bird of prey. No, I don't believe that is registered."

"Good. Register the name Eagles, then."

"Harmond's Eagles." The man mused a moment. "An odd name. And your Captains?"

"As registered," said Gregg hastily. "How is my credit?"

The man glanced at something before him, and shook his head. "Not so good, I'm afraid. Twenty-eight thousand credits. You wish to subscribe to the Information Section?"

"Of course."

"Shall I connect you?"

"Have them send all available information on this sector. I'll record it."

"As you wish," he smiled.

"Good luck, Commander." The screen went blank.

Merry loosed an explosive gasp of relief. "Done it!" He grinned at Fenson and Gregg. "Well, we're in business. Here's to Harmond's Eagles, long may they prey."

They joined him in laughter.

* * * *

The first job was to clean and repair the ships. Gregg insisted, and the others grumblingly agreed that poor ships meant poor crews. For a while the crews scrubbed, polished, oiled and repaired as they had never done before. Gregg spent the last few credits on meagre supplies. The men grumbled, but under the watchful eyes of Fenson and Merry, they worked.

Gradually the ships took on a new air. Some of the sleekness reappeared. Instruments worked, turrets showed clear plastic, the coating of gun-smoke vanished. As the ship improved in appearance, so did the men. Finally Gregg was satisfied.

He called a council of Captains, and over a jug of wine they discussed the next move. Merry was all for action. Fenson agreed, but was more cautious. Gregg knew that he had to get action quickly, or lose his command.

Luck favoured him.

From the information section of the Arsenal came news of action in their sector. A planet, grown greedy, had hired a war group and sent a challenge to a neighbouring world. They had radioed a call for help. Gregg decided to accept.

Within minutes they were in space, then hyper-space. Hours from their destination, Gregg slowed their progress and, made plans.

"This world is attacked by three ships. We've only two. Now, I'll go in with one, and you, Fenton, stay hidden with your ship. They'll think us easy meat. When engaged, you attack. Agreed?"

Merry shook his head. "Can't do it, Gregg. Under the code we must discuss area of combat with the opposing Commander. You see," he explained, "war to us is like a game. Men get killed, sure, but we don't want the thing to hang out too long." He grinned. "Not unless the planets can pay, of course, and these little worlds can't. So we set up an objective, decide on an area, and then wade in."

"There's another way," Fenson said craftily. "No sense in either of us getting hurt if we can help it. Some Commanders are agreeable to an arrangement—maybe this one is. Have a token battle, the richest side loses, and we divide the cash."

"Is that allowed?"

"No. If found out we get kicked out of the Arsenal." Fenson grinned wryly. "That's why Merry and I can't register."

Gregg drummed fingers on the desk before him. "Contact the opposing Commander. Let's see who he is."

It was a scavenger of the Rim who answered the call. A ferret-eyed man, who grinned with relief when he recognised Merry. Fenson nodded to Gregg and held up one hand, the fingers bent in a rough circle.

"Hello, Merry," the ferret-eyed man called. "Glad to see you. Can we talk business?"

"Not yet, Maddock. Call you back, though. I think it'll be O.K."

He turned to Gregg. "I know Maddock. Slippery as a snake, but he'll be agreeable to do things the easy way."

Gregg bit his lip. "I don't like it. He may record, and we'd be paying blackmail from here on." He looked up as an idea struck him. "This Maddock, is he the Commander?"

Merry shrugged. "Says so. Can't prove it though."

"What are his ships like?"

"Not too good. Fast though. A bit smaller than ours. Why?"

"We could use those ships," Gregg mused. "Would his men come over to us?"

"Maybe. Why?"

He slapped his thigh. "I told you that he had brains, Fenson. Think it'll work?"

"I don't get it," complained Fenson. "What've you got in mind?"

Merry chuckled. "Tell you later. Shall I fix it up, Gregg?"

Gregg nodded. "Keep me out of it. Fenson too. We don't want to give him too much on us."

Merry nodded and turned to the radio.

* * * *

The battle was to be on the single small satellite of the challenging world. A beacon had been fixed, and the ships drifted down on opposing sides. Men spilled from them, and the battle was on.

It was a farce. Gregg set off charges, deployed men, made a great deal of fuss and fire. Maddock did the same. To any casual observer it would appear that the two sides were locked in mortal combat.

It had been decided that Maddock should win. Gregg hadn't argued at the proposal, though he knew that the men intended to cheat him. He had his own ideas, two could cheat, though not quite in the same way.

The radio at his ear bleeped, and Merry's voice sounded startlingly close. "All set, Gregg?"

"O.K. Move in. Remember, I want the ships, never mind about killing the men." He waited for ten minutes and called Fenson. "O.K., get moving."

The scene of the battle altered. Gregg's men made a sudden dash and won the beacon. Immediately they set off the signal flare. Sporadic firing burst from the others and several men fell. Gregg cursed, and called Merry.

"Get Maddock. Ask him what the hell he thinks he's doing."

"Maddock here," a voice grated. "Are you crossing me?"

"Let's talk it over," suggested Gregg.

"We've got the beacon. No sense in killing each other off. O.K.?"

"Who the hell are you?"

"Come out and find out."

"O.K. But it better be good." The firing died. Men came from under cover. The two parties met at the site of the beacon.

"I'm Harmond. Commander of the Eagles. What are you crying about?"

"That battle was to go to me. I've got it recorded. Cross me and I'll have you kicked out of the Arsenal."

Gregg forced his face into a blank mask. "What are you talking about?"

"Don't act dumb. I didn't talk to you, but you're responsible for your Captains. I want the decision."

The radio bleeped in Gregg's ear. "O.K. All tied up and tied down. Shall we join you?"

"No. I can handle it."

"What are you muttering about?" Maddock asked suspiciously.

"Look!" Gregg pointed to where Maddock's ships had landed. Delicately balanced on slender jets, they were lifting into the thin air. Maddock stared and screamed a curse.

"You crossing scut!"

Temper overcame him and he clawed at his blaster. Gregg let him get it clear of the holster, then his own hand moved in swift synchronisation. Maddock stared stupidly for a moment, then slumped lifeless to the ground. Gregg smiled and lifted the hand-gun.

"Anyone else have any objections?"

A man muttered, then fell silent as Gregg stared at him. "No? Then listen. I'm taking you over. I've got your ships. You can sign on if you like. I don't need you, but I can use you. If any of you don't like the idea, he's at liberty to go. I'll drop him off at the nearest planet."

He waited, the thin scar on his temple livid against his bronze skin. No one moved. He smiled. "Good. You're in the Eagles now. Harmond's Eagles. The best war-group ever." He spoke in the radio. "Bring them down, Merry."

He grinned. As he had guessed, the sheer audacity of the move had caught them all by surprise. They were stunned now, a little scared. Later, they would talk. He could guess at what they would say.

Merry came up at a run, grinning like a lunatic. He saw Maddock, and looked sharply at Gregg.

"Self-defence," said Gregg calmly. He gestured towards the men. "I've witnesses."

He felt suddenly tired. "Contact the planets, Merry. Collect as much as the traffic will bear. Then get the Arsenal. We must be on the move."

Merry stared in disappointment. "Don't we get any time off, Gregg? That planet will be grateful; we could have some fun."

"I don't kill for fun, Merry. Get moving." He turned away. Merry looked after him, a strange look in his narrowed eyes.

* * * *

The Director smiled ruefully and held out his hand as Gregg entered the office. "Well, Commander, we lost. Negal must pay for her rash excursion into war." He shrugged. "Fortunes of war, of course, but it still isn't nice to take."

Gregg took the proffered hand. "No hard feelings, I hope?"

"None. At least we are civilised." He frowned thoughtfully. "I had heard great things of Maddock. I should have thought he would have put up a better show."

"Maddock is dead," Gregg snapped curtly. "Now to business. You agree that my claim is a fair one?"

"Can I protest? But I must admit that you are very reasonable." His face darkened. "Not so our late enemy. But you will not be concerned with that."

"No," agreed Gregg. "But console yourselves with the thought that you would have been even harder had the war gone otherwise. Have you my payment?

"It is here. Payable to Harmond's Eagles, via hyper-beam to the InterGalactic bank on the Arsenal." He paused, pen in hand, and glanced at Gregg.

"Are you leaving immediately, Commander?"

Gregg smiled as he caught the subtle inflection of the Director's question.

"Not at once," he admitted, and grinned. "Perhaps you had better let me have part of the sum in cash. Fifty thousand I think will be enough to go on with."

The Director smiled and hastily made the adjustment. "You will find the people glad to entertain your men, Commander." He rose from the deep chair. "I trust that you will enjoy your stay."

"I'll send a party for the money. Make it in small bills. It will be easier for your tavern keepers to change."

They smiled at each other, both knowing exactly what was in the other's mind.

Outside a faint wind blew, carrying the promise of snow. Gregg was suddenly reminded of distant Lagos, and felt a pang of nostalgia. It seemed but a short while ago when he and Owen had walked from the newly-arrived rocket, and now? Owen was gone, and he was master of five ships.

He shrugged angrily, and swung in a nearby tavern. The place was full of uniformed men. He could recognize men of both Groups, already hobnobbing, swapping drinks and lies. He grinned. Given a few weeks in the confines of the ships, an engagement or two, and they would united into a solidly loyal body of men.

He nodded to one or two, stood a round of drinks. Told a yarn and cracked a joke, then, because it wasn't policy to encourage too great a familiarity between officers and men, moved on. He repeated the technique in several places, steadily moving across the town towards the landing field. Dim in the gathering dusk, the slender shapes of his rockets rose above the town like spires of some old cathedral city.

The wind had freshened. Suddenly, on one of the stronger gusts, he heard the sound of a roaring song. It came from a nearby tavern, and he paused within the low doorway, watching a well-remembered scene.

Merry sprawled in his best dress uniform, a great pot in one hand, his red face flushed with wine and laughter. Around him clustered the younger element of town—bright-eyed youths, sparkling girls, eager-faced men. They hung on Merry's outrageous lies, and cheered him onto fresh exaggerations.

"Why," he bellowed, "look at me. Silk, gold, adventure, and never a scratch in thirty years of action. Join the Eagles, lads, and come home dripping with wealth. Follow Harmond, the best Commander a Group ever had. I promise you that you'll never regret it. Some there are who've travelled half across the Galaxy to sign on. You're the lucky ones. We're on your very doorstep. Sign now, before you eat your hearts out in vain regret at missing this golden chance."

Gregg smiled ironically. Merry could put on a good show. All over town men were telling tall yarns, buying free drinks, recruiting for the Wargroup. He caught Merry's eyes, jerked his head in a signal. In a few moments, Merry joined him outside.

"How does it go?"

"Couldn't be better. They're almost eating out of my hand. We'll fill our complement here, Gregg."

"Good. We're blasting tomorrow. Have your men on the field just after daybreak."

He returned the other's salute, watched the tavern a moment longer, then turned away. He almost knocked the woman down.

She was, he saw, no longer young, though she had kept her figure and the night was kind to her face. She caught his arm as he muttered an apology.

"Commander?"

"Yes?"

"I want to speak to you. Will you come with me? It isn't far."

"Sorry," he snapped curtly. "Try some other man. I'm busy."

He heard the sharp hiss of her indrawn breath as the import of his meaning struck her, and then a shaky laugh. "I'm not what you seem to think, Commander. It was about another matter."

"What is it?"

"My son. He's in there. I think that he intends to sign on. I want you to stop him."

"Is he of age?" Gregg snapped the question impatiently.

"Yes, but—"

"Then what can I do?" he interrupted rudely.

"Refuse him. Fail him in his tests. Anything, but I beg of you not to take him from me."

Gregg sighed. He had met possessive mothers before. She seemed to know what he was thinking, and spoke in a calmer tone.

"My husband was a Warbird," she murmured. "He met me on Orionus III. I was a taxi dancer. We were happy for a while, money was free and his Group was strong. When Darl was coming he left the Group, and we settled here. We were very happy."

She broke off. In the dim, half-light Gregg could see the tears streaming silently down her cheeks.

"He was never meant to be a farmer. Debts grew, crops failed, one day he left us. I heard from him at times. He sent us money—plenty of money, and then..."

"Which Group did he join?" Gregg asked gently.

"Curlew's Invincibles. They—"

"I know," he interrupted. He did know. They had been caught in a trap, refused to surrender, and had been fried to a man.

"So you understand why I ask you to spare me my son?"

"But if he wants to join...?" Gregg asked helplessly.

"He will. His head is filled with dreams easy conquests, quick riches. He hasn't yet learned that there are two sides to every coin."

"And you have?"

"How many recruits live through the first engagement?" she asked quietly. "I know how they are trained. Under fire. If they die, good riddance. If they live, they have learned, and may live through the next. What is the life expectancy of a Warbird? That man in there, never been scratched he says, then why does he carry the scars of re-graft?"

"That was hardly a scratch," Gregg said mildly. He stood deep in thought. This woman knew too much. If she chose to talk, she could arouse the entire town against them, and they badly needed fresh recruits. One new man just wasn't worth the price.

"Jendara." She caught his sleeve. "Will you...?"

"Your son is safe from me, madam," he said stiffly. "In return you will say nothing?"

"Nothing," she answered gladly. "I promise you."

He nodded, and walked away. Behind him the woman dried her eyes, and watched his broad frame dwindle in the starlight, then turned, and resumed her lonely vigil outside the tavern.

CHAPTER 7

PAID TO FIGHT

Maddock had been rich. Merry gloated over the statement from the Arsenal, and tried to cheer Gregg with the news. "Look! Over two hundred thousand credits! Add the three ships, the spoil from the losing planet, and what we had, and it's the most profitable enterprise I've ever been in. Even cut three ways..."

"What are you talking about? Who said anything about cutting three ways?" Gregg surged to his feet. "Look, Merry, you too, Fenson, let's get this straight. You wanted to go places. You weren't satisfied with a little, you wanted a lot. You killed to get it, and now, so have I. Well, we're going to get it. Not just a few thousand in the bank, but more than you've ever dreamed of."

He paused, rubbing the scar on his temple. Angrily he shook his head. "Listen. We need money, ships and men. I don't want to hang about the Rim all my life. We'll move to the centre. Didn't you say that there is wealth and power there?"

"What's come over you, Gregg?" Merry asked, a thread of anger in his voice. "You've altered. Ever since Owen died, you've not been the same. What's wrong?"

"Nothing. Now get to work. Get these ships as clean as possible. Check everything. Send for supplies. Move, blast you! Do I have to teach you your work?"

Merry flushed and snarled a curse. "Careful, Harmond. Don't get too big. I deposed Alendi, and I can depose you just as easily."

"You think so?" Gregg deliberately slapped the florid features. Merry turned livid, one hand clawed at his blaster, and he almost gibbered with rage.

Gregg watched him contemptuously, as the weapon came clear, he stepped forward and coldly smashed his fist into the cursing mouth. When Merry regained his feet, he looked down the unwavering barrel of a pistol.

"Well?" Gregg smiled coldly. Then in sudden fury: "Are you a fool, Merry? Kill me if you wish, but never threaten. I'm not proud of Alendi's death. But if you think that I'm afraid of you, you'd better think again. Here," he tossed the blaster at Merry, "use it if you think it'll help you."

Deliberately he turned his back.

Fenson caught Merry's arm as he swung up the weapon. "Don't do it, Merry. I tell you, don't!" Then as Merry wavered in doubt, "You did wrong to threaten. I've told you before. You know as well as I do that any successful Group must have discipline. Well, that's what we're getting. Don't you want to get rich?"

"He slapped me!" Merry spat the words. "I'll take that from no man. Let me go, Fenson. This is between Harmond and me."

"Talk to him, Gregg," appealed Fenson. "Gods, if you don't make it up, I'll kill you both." Frantic at the thought of losing the dream of a lifetime, Fenson quivered with sheer rage. "Make it up, I say. Are you both crazy?"

Merry looked at him with surprise. The mark of Gregg's hand stood clear against the red skin. He shook his head in wonderment. "I believe he'd do it."

"I'd do it!" promised Fenson grimly. "Well?"

Gregg turned to Merry and held out his hand. "I apologise." He shrugged. "Nerves, I guess. I'm all keyed up."

Merry dropped his weapon, held out his hand. Gregg took it, smiled, then reeled as Merry's fist swung with immense force against his face.

He leaned against the chart table wiping blood from his split lips. Surprisingly, he grinned. "O.K. Merry. I asked for it. Satisfied?"

"Yeah. Now we're even."

Fenson blew out his breath in a gasp of relief. "Hell," he grunted, "when you've finished playing, how about getting to work?"

* * * *

The next engagement was a second farce. This time Gregg hired half of his forces to each of two opposing sides, played the game of bloodless war, and collected from the richest.

The next wasn't. For the first time he knew the impact of true war. Ships reeled under savage blows. Blood seeped beneath warped doors, air hissed from torn hulls. The roar of the turret became a dirge for the pain-twisted bodies of broken men.

Merry lunged through the smoke of the back-flash of the guns. "Gregg!" he yelled. "Fenson reports two ships riddled and out of action. We're losing air fast. What are your orders?"

"Get all men in suits. Tell Fenson to cease fire, make out that his ship is knocked out. We've got to tempt them in close. They outrange us. Move!"

He returned to the firing board. "Turrets one to three, cease fire. Turrets four to six, fire spasmodically." Half the guns fell silent. Through the screen he could see Fenson's ship suddenly jerk from course, begin a slow, erratic spin.

Gregg watched stiff with tension. Absently he allowed his aide to fetch him a spacesuit, clambered into the stiff fabric, adjusted the flow of oxygen. Would the ruse work?

Before him the visi-screen flashed into life. At the first sign of the incoming call, he slumped across the control board. The triumphant face of the opposing Commander stared from the cleared screen. He looked with triumphant satisfaction at the body slumped across the controls, stared at the carnage seen through the half-opened door. Turning to his aide, he rapped swift orders.

"We've got 'em. Close in. Their Commander's dead. If they don't surrender, blast them from space." He sneered from the safety of his distant cabin. "Poor fool! I've clipped your wings, Warbird." The title was an insult. The screen went blank.

Gregg sprang to his feet. Through the outside vision plates he could see the slender ships of the enemy closing in for the kill.

They outnumbered him two to three, and he envied their sleek deadliness. Late model ships, sprouting guided missile tubes. Built for the roar and fury of interstellar war.

Their Commander was overconfident. Assured that the riddled ships before him could offer no threat now that their Commander was dead, he neglected even the most elementary precautions. He lounged carelessly at his control board, and let his thoughts drift to future pleasures.

Suddenly the seemingly helpless ships sprang to vicious and deadly life. Turrets blazed a hail of snarling death. Fenson's apparently helpless ship, jerked out of the erratic spin, levelled, and blasted with very gun operative. The enemy crumpled.

In his cabin, the opposing Commander leapt to his feet with a startled oath. Orders spat from his lips, and savagely he jerked at the controls. Something smashed against the hull, air whined, a thin shrill sound. Another impact, and the Commander died, still cursing, a bloody froth on his lips as the air in the cabin exploded into the vacuum of space.

Gregg smiled tiredly as the radio brought hasty offers of surrender. Then, as the elation of battle died, reaction set in. He looked dully at the lifeless body of his aide, the blood-stained floor, the wrenched and twisted plates of bulkheads and hull.

Of five ships two were utterly gutted, fit only for salvage. He had lost two-thirds of his men, and over half the remainder had wounds. He himself felt numb, stunned by the ferocity of spatial warfare.

Merry lurched into the control room, stemming blood spouting from a slashed arm. He grinned, the thick coating of greasy dirt cracking over his face as he did so. Despite himself, Gregg had to smile.

"Good work, Gregg. We've got total surrender." He saw Gregg's face.

"Anything wrong?"

"No. I guess not. How's the arm?"

Merry shrugged. "I've had worse." He pursed thick lips. "A hot action, Gregg, for a while I thought that they'd got us. If you hadn't lured them into close quarters, we'd have been dead ducks."

"I guess so," Gregg agreed listlessly. "Fenson O.K.?"

"Sure." Merry chuckled. "Trust the old hands to keep alive. The rookies suffered most." He shrugged carelessly. "What the hell, we can always get more."

"Yeah," said Gregg dully. "We can always get more."

Somehow he kept remembering the woman on Negral. He was glad that he had refused to take her son.

* * * *

They recruited at Jeydrons Landing, and from there moved to Ginna II. Spencerville paid heavily for the pleasure of being beaten, and Gregg added to his strength at Orladdi's fourth planet. He left New Tortuga, a Warbird base, in flaming ruins, and rid three colonies of alien life.

Moving at speed, he cut a path of successful engagements. Several small groups he utterly absorbed, giving them the quick choice of surrender or destruction. Contrary to general practice he always took both ships and credits of his beaten opponents. This was against all custom and usage of the Rim Groups, where a rough system of 'live and let live' had long been the rule.

Inevitably he grew rich. Inevitably he gained a reputation for utter ruthlessness. He now took only selected men, hardened veterans of many battles. He imposed strict discipline. Poured wealth into the finest equipment and weapons. Among the Commanders of the many little Wargroups operating along the Rim, his name became hated.

They feared him, and in direct measure of their fear, hated. To oppose him was to invite certain defeat. Wargroups which had scavenged among the poorer worlds, fighting half-hearted war, or hiring out as exterminators, knew that at any moment Harmond's Eagles might oppose them.

They lied about him, but there was a grain of truth in their lies. He cheated, took every advantage of wealth and reputation, lured their best men, even offered sanctuary to those who deserted. Like a ravening scourge he swept along the edge of the Galaxy, and none could oppose him.

Merry grew worried. He confided his fears to Fenson one day when both were on watch. They wore impeccable uniforms of shimmering black cellosilk, liberally adorned with gold piping. On the left breast they bore Harmond's insignia—an Eagle, wings half-spread, cruel beak open as if to emit a raucous cry.

"How far are we going, Fenson?" He wasn't talking about parsecs or other lineal measurement.

Fenson shrugged. "Who knows? Gregg maybe. I don't." He grinned sardonically. "What's the matter, Merry? Getting worried?"

"Aren't you? Look at the position we're in. Hated." He mused thoughtfully. "I've never been so hated before. Disliked, yes, but always I've known that I'd be acceptable to any Group. Now? They'd shoot me on sight."

"You're exaggerating," said Fenson uneasily. "It's not that bad."

"No? What about that last engagement? Baxter's Battlers I think they were. As soon as they knew who they were up against they yielded by default. Took off into hyper-space without firing a shot."

"They were crazy. They'll be blacklisted all over the Galaxy."

"So what? If they'd fought they would have lost everything. As it is, they can sell the ships, hire out, amalgamate; a dozen things. Anyway, they're still alive." Merry kicked savagely at the bulkhead.

"Never mind," Fenson consoled. "Think of all the money you've got."

"What money?" Merry gestured towards the ship. "This is my money. Today I'm worth more than I ever dreamed of, tomorrow I may have a part share in a heap of junk."

"But we've still got millions banked at the Arsenal," protested Fenson uneasily.

"Maybe we have, but what if Gregg takes it into his head to buy more ships? Where's our ready cash then?" Merry spat. "I may be worth millions, but can I enjoy it? Can I hell! Leaping about like a flea on a blanket all the time. Look at that last world. I could have enjoyed myself there. Did we stay? Two days. Two stinking days—and half that time I was recruiting." He swore feelingly.

A uniformed man came up to them, saluted smartly and stood stiffly at attention. Merry glowered at him. "Well?"

"Commander Harmond's respects, sir. He requests your presence on the bridge."

Merry grunted. "O.K."

"Yes, sir." He saluted again spun sharply on his heel, and marched smartly away. Merry stared morosely after him. "Even old Alendi wasn't as bad as this. A man could relax on his ship. Now, even the officers have to dress like a lot of parade-ground toy soldiers."

Fenson pulled at his arm. "Let's go and see what he wants."

"Some crazy scheme, I suppose," grumbled Merry. "It nearly always is." He slouched his way to the bridge, Fenson grinning behind him.

* * * *

Gregg rose as they entered, and gestured for his aide to leave them alone. He had aged since leaving Lagos. Young though he was, yet his hair showed traces of grey. Lines showed at the corners of eyes and mouth, and his features bore a stamp of hard ruthlessness at odds with the youthful suppleness of his body.

He had seen too much death. Too many battles. Too much deep concentration and worry, with too little relaxation. Now, some of the burden seemed to slip from his shoulders. He smiled, and for a moment the young and eager farmer from far Lagos showed through the iron shell.

He grasped Merry's hand, and nodded cheerfully to Fenson. When they were seated he lifted a slender jar of wine, and poured three goblets full. He grinned at Merry's stare of recognition.

"Surprised?" He held his goblet to the light, admiring the deep ruby glow of the thick wine. "It seems a long time ago when we three sat at a table drinking this wine and making plans. I made a promise then; have I kept it?"

Merry gulped wine, and nodded. "Better than we had any right to expect."

Gregg laughed. "You thought to use me, didn't you?" He raised a hand at their protestations. "Don't deny it. I'd have been a fool not to have guessed." He sighed, gently rotating the goblet. "A lot has happened since then. We are the strongest Group in this part of the Galaxy, the strongest outside the Centre. Too strong. No one will fight us."

"You can't blame them," grumbled Merry. "They haven't a chance. You always win and then strip them clean. What else did you expect?"

"What I've got—the strongest Wargroup ever known to this part of the Galaxy." He settled back in the big chair, smiling reminiscently. "From a tatter of single ships, tiny Groups able only to scavenge, to bicker among themselves. I have built this great war machine. I built it for a purpose. Those Captains I stripped, they won't regret it. They are serving beneath, I'll see they win treble what they lost."

"How?" Fenson leaned forward eagerly. "There's no further pickings on the Rim. You've stripped it clean. There's not a Group left that dare opposes us. What are your plans?"

Gregg looked understandably at Fenson. "I see that you've grasped the essentials. As you say we cannot stay on the Rim. The time has come for decision."

Merry set down his goblet and frowned. "I don't get it. What must we decide?"

"Whether or not to sell out, retire on what we have, or to seek fields to conquer. You are partners in this with me. You gave me my start, such as it was. It is for you to decide." He leaned back, toying with his wine.

For a long time the argument raged back and forth. Fenson, fired with ambition, was for expansion. Merry, greedy though he was, wanted to hold onto what they had. Gregg summed it up for him.

"We cannot stay here as we are. Have you any idea of what it costs to keep the Group intact? We're spending millions every week in pay alone. To get it we must have work. Engagements, employment from wealthy planets. There aren't any big enough on the Rim to support us. If we won't decide, then the men will desert through lack of pay. The Captains will resign. We'll be left with a hollow shell of a Wargroup, and nothing to operate it with."

"Can't we keep a smaller Group?"

"No!" Gregg's eyes blazed with fury. "I've built this Group from nothing. If it goes, all of it goes. I'll be second to none."

"But what can we do in the centre?" Merry looked worried.

"There's work there. The Tri-Combine, the Amalgamated, the Independents, Wargroups who are at continual war. We could ask for our own price. Empires, swollen with wealth, greedy with expansion. A hundred potential dictators. I tell you, man, we'll roll in wealth." His eyes sparkled at the prospects.

"He's right, Merry," Fenson agreed, his ugly face glowing with inner ambition. "Why stop now?"

"I'm not sure." Merry tugged at his ear in perplexity. "I've seen Warbirds come and go before. They got greedy. Took on more than they could handle, went up in smoke."

"Not all of them." Gregg smiled. "I've heard you talk of others. What of those Groups who won planets, empires?"

"By Space, he's right, Merry!" Fenson clapped a hand on the fat man's shoulder. "Remember Einar? Swenson? O'Brian? Remember them? They took a chance and look where it got them. O'Brian founded a dynasty. Swenson sold out and bought himself a pleasure system. Einar lords it over three suns and fifteen planets. Isn't the game worth it? Wasn't that what we always wanted?"

Merry sprang to his feet in excitement, the little eyes gleaming with lust for power. "I'm with you," he roared. "All the way. A quick end, or wealth, power, all the loot of the Centre." Fired now, he was more eager than Fenson.

Gregg watched them, smiling with secret thoughts. Filling the goblets he raised one high above his head. "A toast," he demanded. "To the Eagles and success."

"To the Eagles," they roared," and success!"

The empty goblets spattered against the bulkhead.

CHAPTER 8

THE BARBARIANS

The blaster spat a livid tongue of flame across the clearing, something stirred, broke into a desperate run crashing through the undergrowth. The blaster spat again, a bush burst into flame, something screamed a high animal cry of agony. A third jet of flame, and silence.

Incongruously a woman laughed, a high-pitched trilling, devoid of all emotion but casual amusement.

"Why, Paul! Three shots! And you a professional!"

Her companion flushed and thrust the jewelled weapon back into its holster. "You may laugh, Selene, but if it were a ship I aimed at, one shot would suffice."

She smiled at the tall figure, and laid a slender hand on his arm. "I don't doubt it, Paul. I would not have it otherwise, else how could any of us rest easy in our beds?"

He looked at her sharply, sensing mockery, but the oval face wreathed in hair of deepest jet, showed nothing but concern. He squinted at the darkening sky. "It grows late. Perhaps we had better return." He turned to the attendants and gave curt orders. They bowed, and hastened to gather the equipment of the hunt.

He made a fine figure as he stood snapping orders. Tall, the lithe body was trimly clad in a uniform of scarlet and gold. Jewels picked out his insignia. On his left breast he bore a device resembling a clenched fist, the device of the Amalgamateds, of whom he was local Commander.

He sensed her gaze and turned, smiling. "May a humble Commander request the company of Selene of Botan on a walk to her father's palace?"

"I doubt it if the Lord of Botan would consider it remiss if the Commander of his armed forces escorted his daughter." They both laughed, and side by side commenced the journey through the glades to the palace.

For a while they walked in silence, he stealing glances at her flawless features, but she kept her eyes to the path and appeared not to notice. An animal, suddenly dashing from concealment, made them both start. Self-consciously he unholstered his weapon, the too-handsome features, stamped with the look of inborn arrogance, flushing with annoyance.

"Afraid of the Barbarians, Paul?" Mockery tinged the clear voice.

He snorted. "Those tattermadalions? If they dared to venture into the Centre they wouldn't last a single engagement. Who would be fool enough to employ them?"

"Some have," she answered softly. "Lord Pearson won three worlds with their aid. The Tri-Combine is still licking its wounds."

"A fluke. A lucky chance. A poor Commander." He gestured angrily. "They should have been wiped out."

"But they weren't, and Lord Pearson doubled his empire." She smiled enviously.

"He will lose it," promised Paul. "Already the Independents are snarling at his heels."

"But they dare not attack. Didn't they lose a wing of fifteen to those same Barbarians?" She paused. "Paul. Have you thought over what we spoke about a week ago?"

He shifted uncomfortably and stared straight before him. "I told you, Selene. It can't be done."

"But why not? Haven't we right on our side? Within my own memory Botan has lost two thirds of its empire. Why can't we win it back?"

"There is a mutual pact between all Groups of the Amalgamated. You know that. If there weren't, Botan would have been lost years ago."

"So you take our money and give only token services." Her voice was bitter.

"Not so. If there were no pact, then your treasury could never afford to hire a Wargroup strong enough to defend you. As things are, you keep what you have, but so do all others protected by the Amalgamated."

"And if we should hire another Group?"

"Then Botan would be ruined." He turned to her. "Listen to me, Selene. I know of your ambition, but it is a mad, hopeless one. You arc living a dream. Who could you hire? Who would be prepared to fight the entire might of the Amalgamated, or the Tri-Combine, or even the Independents?" He shook his head. "There is a balance of power here in the Centre, and it is a good thing. Wars there can be, and will be, but it is the Wargroups who will decide."

"Cowards!" she spat.

"No. Realists. Like it or not, it is the Wargroups who rule the Galaxy." Arrogance rode every word. "Your petty little quarrels mean nothing to us. We look after our men."

"How dare you speak like this? Are you mad? You, a paid mercenary, to address the daughter of a Lord of Empire as an equal?" She gave a scornful laugh.

He smiled. "Selene, don't be a fool. If I wished, I could leave your Empire defenceless to the first man with money enough to hire a Wargroup to take it for him." Anger darkened his features. "Your insults I can stand. Your blind stupidity I cannot. My wife must have at least the elements of common sense."

"Your wife?" Sheer amazement at his effrontery sent her almost speechless. "I? Your wife?"

"Why not? Why do you think I have spoken so freely?" He caught her hand. "Selene, darling. I know how you feel. Since I first took up this command, I have known that you were the only one I could wish to sit at my side. As my wife your interests would be mine. We could recapture your lost empire. Enlarge it. It can easily be arranged."

"By your precious balance of power, I suppose?" she sneered.

"And who, or what, is there to break it?"

"The Barbarians," she snapped, caution forgotten in her desire to injure. "Harmond's Eagles if you have forgotten the name."

He laughed, genuinely amused. "That scum? That collection of scavengers from the Rim? And how will you hire them? With kisses?"

"Perhaps." She smiled thinly, secretly.

They walked in silence.

* * * *

Selid, Lord of Botan, was an old man. Thin, stooped, white-haired, yet with eyes still burning with the fires of youth. He sat in a deep chair, and with his own hands poured wine for his guest.

Gregg smiled his thanks, lifted his glass, and sipped delicately at the pale, golden wine. Setting it down, he stared at his host through narrowed eyes.

"When you sent for me I had my doubts. Now I still have them. Why did you ask me to call secretly, alone?"

Selid pursed his thin lips and busied himself with the wine. "I would like to hear of your battle which won Lord Pearson three worlds."

Gregg shrugged. "We fought. We won."

"I..." Selid hesitated. "You know of the situation here in the Centre?"

"Is there one?"

"Yes. I..." He hesitated again, fumbling at his glass.

Gregg leaned forward. "Maybe it would be as well if you were frank with me," he suggested. "I have no time for the playing of games. Naturally your confidences will be respected." He sat back, sipping at the wine.

Selid pulled at his lip, then with a wry smile nodded his head. "Very well, though what I say must be forever between us. Is that agreed?"

Gregg nodded impatiently. "How often must I say it?"

Selid flushed. The Lord of Botan was accustomed to rather more deference than he was receiving. He swallowed his temper. "For years I have been paying the Amalgamated for protection. It is a token payment, a retainer fee for immediate aid if and when I need it. It does not include service for attack. Only defence."

"So?"

"Once Botan held three suns and twenty-three planets in her empire. Now we are but a third of that. I am an old man, but the memory of that shameful defeat rankles still. I would be avenged."

"You want to attack, recapture your lost empire, is that it?"

"Yes."

"Then why don't you?"

"Because the Amalgamated have also sold protection to my enemies."

"Then hire another Wargroup—the Tri-Combine, the Independents, anyone." Gregg poured wine and looked his disgust.

"I can't. First, because if I did, the Amalgamated would immediately leave me defenceless, and then would attack on behalf of the other side. Secondly, the three great Wargroups have a pact of mutual non-aggression, and none other is available. Finally, I can't pay them enough."

Gregg climbed to his feet. "The last reason is the one I'm interested in. Good-day, Selid." He moved towards the door.

"Wait!" Moving with surprising speed the old man caught at his arm. "You don't understand. Wargroups believe that they are the real rulers of the Galaxy. They refuse to fight if it doesn't suit them. Rather, they demand so much that no empire could ever pay the sum asked."

He slumped back into his chair. "There's a balance of power in the Centre, and it's the death of enterprise. How can an empire expand, a world right a wrong, if the Wargroups refuse to fight? They sit like spiders, fattening themselves on token payments from a dozen worlds."

Gregg nodded understandingly. Something of such nature had been tried on the Rim. He had thought of it himself, but it was impracticable for lack of opposition.

He could visualise the set-up. In effect the Wargroups had founded a dynasty. Command would become hereditary. The original purpose of the Wargroups would become lost, and by superior arms they would enforce their will on the entire Galaxy.

He had wondered at the ease of his victories. Now he understood. Once hard men, men who had lived by war, had become soft, had taken the easy way of arbitration, adjustments, instead of the snarling of guns. They had forgotten how to fight!

"You could break that balance," Selid, wise with years of Court intrigue, insinuated the suggestion craftily.

"How?"

"Ally yourself with one or the other of the Wargroups, sow dissension, and attack when the time is ripe."

"And restore your empire in the process?"

"Naturally." Selid grinned mirthlessly. "I offer big prizes. I stake all I own. Well?"

Gregg sat for a moment, deep in thought. It sounded attractive. Selid, he knew, was utterly self-seeking, but two could play at that game, and he did need an employer.

"How much can you offer?"

Hope flared in the old man's eyes. "You accept?"

"Provisionally. I must discuss it in Council."

Selid frowned. "But I thought that you were sole Commander?"

"I am," Gregg grinned." But a wise man shares the work—and the blame." He rose to his feet. "You'll be hearing from me. Until then continue as normal. Agreed?"

"Agreed." Selid held out his hand, all thoughts of superior rank forgotten.

Abruptly the door of the room crashed open.

Selene stared with unashamed curiosity at the man with her father. Tall, with a supple figure, hinting of wiry strength. Black hair swept back from a high forehead. A scar traced a livid passage across the left temple, adding, rather than detracting, from his masculine charm. Eyes narrowed and cold, stared back at her.

He wore no uniform, but the bearing, the unconscious alertness of his entire carriage, stamped him as one different to others. Mentally she compared him with Paul, and somehow Paul suffered by comparison.

In return Gregg stared at the haughty beauty framed in the doorway. Her head came about level with his chin, yet though tall, she had lost none of the soft curves of womanhood. Jet hair framed an oval face, breathtaking in its sheer perfection, and in every movement she betrayed a half-conscious arrogance of rank and birth.

For a long moment they stood staring, and Selid, seeing the sudden interest Gregg displayed, smiled and was secretly pleased.

"My daughter," he introduced. "Selene, a visitor from the Rim."

Lashes fluttered demurely as she smiled at the tall Commander. "I am pleased to see you, and would it be presumptuous to hope that I may see you again?"

"Perhaps." Gregg forced himself to be curt. "Our next meeting must depend on many things. But this I may confess. What man can do to speed it, that I will do." He bowed, a stiff inclination of the head, and left them alone.

Outside, he hastened to the landing field and the small ship that had brought him from where his fleet waited. Half running down a shaded path, he bumped heavily into a man walking in the opposite direction. Gregg staggered, caught his balance, and turned to apologise.

One glance told him who his companion was. The scarlet uniform, the jewelled insignia—that and the blistering curse, stamped the Warbird. Gregg became humble, all haste forgotten.

"A thousand pardons, sir, for my clumsiness. Are you hurt?"

"No," Paul snapped. Then looked closer at Gregg. "I haven't seen you before. Who are you?"

"A stranger. I had hoped to find employment here, but Lord Botan tells me that I must return to the Rim to find it."

"Oh?" Paul narrowed his eyes. "What employment did you seek?"

Gregg gestured. "I fought with the Warbirds. Alendi, Maxwell, Harmond. I—"

Eagerly Paul interrupted. "Harmond? The Eagles?"

"Yes. I served a term, but resigned."

"Why?"

Gregg shrugged. "I had ambition. Also I have ethics. Harmond didn't satisfy either."

Paul stood thinking for a moment. This chance was too good to miss. Anything he could learn about the Eagles would be welcomes at Group H.Q. He smiled, and caught hold of Gregg's arm. "Maybe I could help you. You know who I am?"

"Your name, no. But I know that you are a Commander of the Amalgamateds." Gregg felt safe confessing such knowledge. It would be expected that a Warbird would know the insignia of rank, and the devices of the various Wargroups. He put a pleading note in his voice. "I am a good gunner, sir, can navigate too. If I hadn't married, resigned to settle down, I would have had already my own ship. Harmond promised me that."

"Why do you seek work?"

"My wife died. I know no other life."

"I see." Paul stepped towards the palace, then hesitated. "I think that you had better come to my ship. I want to talk with you." The less Selene knew of this meeting, the better. "Our complement is full at the moment, but I can probably find you a place in a friendly Group."

He led the way towards the landing field.

Gregg stared about him with undisguised interest as Paul entered his ship. One of three, it formed a permanent garrison, and Gregg could understand Selid's desire to get rid of them. Such a force must bite deep into his treasury.

He was surprised to find that the ship, though clean and trim, lacked many of the most modern offensive and defensive devices common on his own. He ventured a question.

"This is one of our most modern vessels," replied Paul haughtily. "The Amalgamateds are large enough and strong enough to crush any opponent." He threw open a door. A uniformed youngster leapt to his feet. "Wine," Paul ordered. "I wish to entertain a guest."

Gregg allowed himself to be questioned, clumsy though the questioning was. He drank deep, and seemed to grow careless. Yes, he knew Harmond. A little, ugly man with a coward's soul. Number of ships? They had twenty when he had left, old hulls mostly, and a half piratical crew. Equipment? Old, half of it unreliable. They had to recruit after every engagement. Lives were cheap with the Eagles.

As he drank and babbled, he watched. He began to doubt, then the explanation came to him, and he grinned. Paul was a figurehead! A soft garrison job; a few ships for show, and that was all. He could follow the logic. The Commanders had dipped too deeply into the funds for their own good. Money which should have paid for new equipment had been spent on personal uses.

It was inevitable in any balance of power. There was no need for the Wargroups to constantly invest, and reinvest their credit on replacements, ammunition, and men. They had arrived at a stasis. Income balanced—more than balanced— necessary expenditure. So the officers lived at a higher and higher rate. No battles were being fought. Mutual adjustments, a little give and take, a gentleman's agreement. The Centre Wargroups were living on sheer prestige!

Gregg grinned, and hid his face in his wine. They were ripe for the plucking! The Eagles could strike!

CHAPTER 9

AMALGAMATED DEFEAT

The hyper-beam radio hummed, and on the vision screen a picture began to form. A man stared coldly at them, and Merry whistled with amazement.

"He did it! Chief of the Tri-Combine himself! I thought that old Wendle had died years ago."

Gregg frowned him to silence, and leaned forward to face the screen. "Are we on a fully protected beam?"

"We are." The cold eyes stayed emotionless, the face scarred, ruthless, framed in sparse white hair, reflecting the innate savagery of a nature that had chosen warfare as a mode of life.

Gregg nodded. "You know me?"

"I do."

"I have a proposition to make to you. Are you interested in hearing it?"

"If I were not, would I have granted audience on protected beam?" Wendle frowned. "Get to the point, man."

"I am invading the Centre. I have found employment and I attack very soon. I know of your balance of power and I know that I could never hope to defeat the combined might of all three Wargroups. Will you agree to remain neutral?"

"Who are you attacking?"

Gregg hesitated, but he couldn't keep the secret much longer anyway. "The Amalgamateds."

"I see." The fierce features became wrapped in thought. "And if you defeat them?"

"I will take their place in your balance of power."

"And if I come to their aid?"

"I will fight you both as long as I possibly can. You know what that will mean."

Wendle nodded. "The Independents will take the opportunity to strike. Once weakened, we could offer little resistance." He looked up suddenly. "Have you contacted them?"

Gregg smiled, but said nothing.

"Give me a day to decide," Wendle asked. "There are others to consult."

"A day, then, no more." Pride rang in Gregg's voice. "I ask no man twice, you understand?"

Wendle nodded. The screen went dark, and Merry loosed his breath in an explosive roar.

"Hell, Gregg, what'll you do if he turns you down?"

"He won't. He daren't." Gregg smiled. "I've got him, and he knows it. Together, they and the Amalgamateds could wreck us, but if they did then the Independents will step in. Neither side dares let the other gain an edge."

Fenson bit his lip. "Are you certain, Gregg? Are you sure that Paul didn't know you, and put on an act?"

"If he did, it was a good one. I saw their ships, I tell you. Junk! Even if it was a good bluff, I still think I'm right. History proves it. Any nation, culture, tribe, based and geared for warfare, must continue fighting or fall into decadence. The ancient Spartans, the Romans, the Greeks, when they tried to live peacefully they failed. When the Barbarians attacked, they were helpless. They had forgotten how to fight."

He looked round, grinning. "We are the Barbarians. We shall cut them down by sheer ferocity. Wendle knows it. All the older Commanders know it. They came up the hard way, and they've seen their Wargroups grow soft under peace. To save themselves they must ally themselves with us."

Merry shook his head. "It's a desperate gamble, Gregg."

"It's a mighty prize, Merry. We started with a couple of wrecks on the Rim. Now we stand to win the whole Galaxy! A long way, Merry. A high climb, but we've made it!"

"Maybe," grumbled Merry. "A high climb as you say, but it can be a mighty big fall if we lose."

"Yes." Gregg grew thoughtful. "Are we ready to go, Merry?"

"As far as we can be. The Arsenal dropped the last of the supplies this morning."

"Good. Then move in. We attack at once."

"Are you crazy?" Fenson caught Gregg's arm. "What about Wendle? Aren't you going to wait to hear from him?"

"No!" Angrily Gregg freed his arm. "Attack now! We'll make up his mind for him."

Behind him Merry, his florid features alight at the prospect of action, bent over the screen as he issued orders.

* * * *

Through hyper-space they slid, swooping like the Eagles they wore, and like Eagles they struck. Ships reeled. Guns flamed. Men died in the vastness of space, spewing up their lives in red-stained foam. Slim shapes became jagged wreckage. Neat uniforms ripped, tore, turned into smouldering rag.

Frantically the Amalgamated poured ships and men into the area. Against the war-hardened veterans of a hundred engagements, the peace-softened Warbirds of the defenders had no chance. But they fought, they could do nothing else.

Gregg conducted operations from his control room, in his flagship. The Group had grown far too big for him to be able both to lead and fight. He followed the reports, his face growing more and more strained as time passed.

Would the reinforcements never stop? He had only a limited force, but the Amalgamated seemed to have unlimited ships. Even though poor fighting material, yet numbers made them dangerous. Merry's face appeared on the screen. "Gregg!"

"Yes?"

"They refuse to surrender." He wiped a rill of blood from over one eye. "What'll we do?"

"What can we do?" snarled Gregg. "Blast them to hell." He cleared the screen. "Get me the Chief Commander of the Independents," he snapped to the operator.

The connection took a long time to make, then just as he was about to cancel the call, a face grinned at him from the screen.

"You wanted to speak to me, Harmond?"

Massine was a wizened little man with the greedy face and darting eyes of a monkey. Elected leader of the combined Group comprising the Independents, his tenure was a precarious one. He squinted at Gregg, the thin, wide mouth writhing with amusement.

Gregg was curt. "I'm wiping out Amalgamated, and I've an idea that Tri-Combine has lent them ships and men. If I'm beaten, then they will unite and wipe you out. They've got to. Either of them alone will be too weak to stand against you. If you come in with me now, we can share the loot between us. Well?"

Massine grinned sardonically. "Sure of yourself, aren't you, Harmond? I'll sit this one out, if you don't mind." He laughed.

From the desk before him a local visi-screen clamoured for Gregg's attention. Irritably he closed a switch. Fenson's face peered through a coating of grime and smoke at him. "Gregg?"

"What is it?"

"Their Commander wishes to offer surrender. What terms?"

"None, and keep blasting till they yield. Take the surrender yourself." He pressed buttons.

"General orders to all units of the Fleet. Prevent any ship leaving the area. Prevent destruction of any ship within the area. That is all." He leaned back, feeling for the first time in days a flood of relief. He had been right. They had won!

He became aware of Massine's startled features still squinting from the visi-screen. He grinned. "You had your chance, Massine. Still want to sit this one out?

The thin lips writhed in anger and fear. "Blast you, Harmond. You've busted a soft racket with your meddling. Why don't you get the hell out of here and back to the Rim?"

Gregg laughed softly. "Maybe I will, Massine—maybe I will. But I'll clean up this part of the Galaxy first. Rid it of scum like you who hold a pistol to the heads of decent people." Anger suddenly choked him. "Scum, parasites, fattening on greed and hate and fear. What chance have people got? What chance for progress when gunmen rule? I'll go— and be glad to go—but I'll go over your rotten, dead bodies."

Massine stared at him in startled amazement. All trace of vicious humour gone. "Are you crazy?" he gasped. "You're a Warbird yourself! What's the difference?"

Gregg snapped the connection without answering. He thought of the victory, of Selene, and strangely he thought of a dead man's sister. He thought of Jean.

* * * *

Selid, Lord of Botan, grinned, and rubbed thin hands together in ill-concealed impatience. The great audience hall of his palace barely held the assembled crowd who had come to watch the surrender of the conquered worlds.

For the hundredth time he peered over the heads of the people below him from the vantage of his dais, but of Harmond there was no sign. He whispered his doubts to Selene, radiant in cloth of gold, standing beside him.

"Do you think he will come?"

She shrugged, and smiled sleepily. "He will come, but would it matter if he didn't?"

"Perhaps not," he agreed. "After all, he is only a hired mercenary; it must be left to his superiors to decide on terms."

She smiled, not answering, and let her gaze drift over the colourful assembly. Bright cellosilk mingled with sober business suiting. Several petty rulers with their attendants, some adventurers, a sprinkling of would-be sycophants eager to fawn on the famous Harmond, or his patron, the Lord of Botan.

Outweighing the civilians were the uniformed Warbirds. Scarlet and gold of the defeated Amalgamateds. Dour faced, grim, angry looking at their sudden downfall. The bright lemon of the Tri-Combine, bearing the interlaced circles of their insignia. The green and orange of the Independents. Search as she might, nowhere could she catch a glimpse of the black and gold of the victorious Eagles.

A deep-voiced command sounded from outside the hall. The clash of weapons, the tread of marching feet, and a file of men forced their way through the crowd to the dais.

A sigh echoed from the assembly. The grim-faced men, weapons swinging at side, trim in their uniforms of black and gold, needed no introduction. Even without the rampart Eagle which each man bore, they would have been known. The Eagles! Harmond had arrived!

He strode lithely through the passage formed by his men. Bareheaded, the scar showing plainly against the white skin, he seemed to have eyes for but one person in the room. Selene felt the impact of his gaze, and smiled. Gregg halted before her father.

"My felicitations, Selid. Are we all assembled?"

Selid flushed. "Your payment is ready," he snapped curtly. "A private room is available for the essential business of reward."

Gregg smiled, and turned to the men behind him. "My Captains, Merry and Fenson," he introduced. "I hope that the Commander of the Amalgamated is here, together with the late rulers of the defeated worlds?"

"They are assembled," Selid snapped. He felt a desire to belittle this man. Within himself—though he would never admit it—he felt an awareness of guilt. He had used this man, now he wanted to be rid of him.

Gregg stepped to his Captains and whispered, "You know what you have to do. Get both Wendle and Massine to agree to an interview. Neither is to know of the other, of course. O.K.?"

Merry winked, and Fenson grinned. "Leave it to us, Gregg." He nodded towards the dais. "Giving them a shock? I like the look of the girl, but don't let her throw you. You know what they really think of us, don't you?"

Gregg nodded, and followed Selid into the private room.

He stopped in surprise at the sight of the uniformed man, then smiled with pleased recognition. "Paul! So you got through it alive. Good." He looked about him. "Where is the Commander?"

"I am the Commander," Paul snapped. "As the highest ranking officer the Command falls on me." He bit his lip. "What are your terms, Harmond?"

"Total surrender. Your ships, credits, supplies, all to become mine."

"No!" Selene rose and stood behind Paul's chair. "That isn't decent. You can't strip him merely because you don't like him."

"Oh?" Gregg stared at her, and understanding came. "So you love him," he said quietly, and laughed a little. "After your hyper-beam messages, your promises, your undying affection?" He shrugged. "No matter. Love affairs via radio are always delicate things; but you enlarge your own importance. It is my custom to take all. I demand what is my right."

"But you will ruin him."

"He would have ruined me," Gregg reminded. "What troubles you, Paul? Aren't you man enough to stand defeat? Or does a woman's skirts soften a Warbird to a snivelling child?"

"By Space, no man talks to me like that!" Paul lunged to his feet, one hand leaping to his holster. As the weapon slid free, Gregg fired. He stood stone-faced, legs slightly astride, the still-smoking weapon hanging loosely from his fingers. He stared down at the crumpled man, at the sobbing woman bent over him. He turned to Selid.

"He will live," he said coldly. "I do not murder, but my terms stand. Selid, find another Wargroup. I've made you an empire. I can take it the same way."

"No!" Sense came to the aged ruler too late. Suddenly he could see what was going to happen to him. To keep what he had would utterly ruin his already depleted treasury. Enemies, jealous of his sudden rise to power, would snarl at his heels, and he had lost the one man who could have kept them at bay.

"No!" he gasped. "She is but a child, Harmond, and who would revenge themselves on a child? Paul has been her friend for years. You can't desert me now. I gave you your chance in the Centre. Do you forget that?"

"You thought to use me, Selid, and you did—but only because I wished it. Now you do as I say, or I'll desert you. Well?"

"Anything." Selid sweated with relief. "I'll never let you down, Harmond, I swear it. You can rely on me to the very end, whatever that will be."

"The end?" Gregg smiled. "Who knows?" He swung on his heel towards the door. "I'll let you know, Selid, but remember, I'm still a free Wargroup, on sale to the highest bidder."

He could still hear the sobbing as the door closed behind him, and for a moment emotion twisted his features. He leaned against the wall, and rested his aching head. A weight pulling at his hand made him glance down in idle wonderment. He still gripped the blaster, and with an angry gesture he thrust it back into the holster. When he re-entered the assembly room he was as normal.

He stood the compliments, the offers of employment, the flattery, as long as he politely could, then with a curt excuse took his leave. Merry met him on the way to the landing field where his ships towered like a forest of spires.

"O.K., Gregg?"

"Yes. And you?"

"As ordered." Merry fell into step beside him. "How's the girl?"

Gregg laughed curtly. "Well, I suppose."

Merry glanced at him sharply, and bit his lip. "Remember Prokeen?" he asked. "Remember what happened after you contacted that other girl of yours? You felt pretty low then, but you got over it. You'll get over this one the same way."

"You think so?" Gregg asked dully.

"Sure of it." The fat face wrinkled one eye, closing in a wink. "Come on, shipmate, let's find a tavern."

"Why not?" Gregg shrugged. They turned into a low doorway, and for the first time in almost five years Gregg got drunk.

CHAPTER 10

APPEAL FOR HELP

Through a cloud of whirling snow the ship drifted down as lightly as if it were another snowflake. The hot gases from the swollen tubes blasted the drifts to steam, clearing a wide patch of the landing field, then, hissing slightly, rested on the wet ground.

Merry squinted through a port and grunted with pleasure. "Right on the nose. I knew that I'd find it first go." He grinned at the pilot. "In the old days we'd have had half the town to welcome us." He laughed. "Last time I was here they would have given us a twelve-gun salute—all aimed at the ship." He spat. "May as well get it over with. Stay alert, I won't be too long—if I am, then come and get me."

The pilot touched his cap. "Yes, sir. About how long shall I wait?"

"Couple of hours, then use your discretion."

He shivered a little as he reached the foot of the ramp, and kicked disgustedly at the snow fringing the field. It took a little while for him to locate the path, then memory returned, and he strode confidently forward. It was winter, and snow began to gently drift from the night sky.

He reached the main street of the small town without seeing anyone, and stopped, frowning. Things had altered slightly. A fire seemed to have destroyed several houses, the raw, smoke-blackened timbers stood among the white, mantel-like bones. The street, too, had changed. It was wider—or maybe memory had played tricks.

He hesitated, then stepped within a doorway at the sound of approaching footsteps. As they reached him he stepped forward, and gripped a slight figure by an arm.

"What...?"

"Take it easy," grumbled Merry. "I'm looking for someone. Do you know an Elder with a daughter named Jean? I don't know his name, but he had a son—Owen, I think the name was. Do you know him?"

"Last house on the right." The figure squirmed free. "Why?"

"Beat it!" snapped Merry. "Here." He flung a gold piece at the man's feet. Before he had found it, Merry had lost himself in the darkness.

The house was a small one, rude timbers caulked with mud, heavily shuttered windows, a solid door. Merry banged on it with his fist, then growing impatient, used the butt of his blaster.

A light gleamed, slippered feet shuffled towards the door, a bar grated. "Who is it?"

"A friend," grunted Merry. "Let me in. I'm freezing."

The door swung wide. Merry stared at a gaunt, thin-faced oldster, shivering in the bitter wind. He stared at Merry for a long moment, studying him by the light of a lantern clutched in one hand. Merry cursed.

"Think I'm a monster? Let me in, man. Do you want us both to freeze?"

Slowly the man stepped aside. "Who are you?" he asked, unbarring the door.

"Have you a daughter named Jean? Had you a son named Owen?" Merry was curt.

"I have. I did." The old man stared hard at Merry. "Now I know you. You are the Warbird who stole our youth from us. My son..." He sobbed and suddenly leapt at the Warbird.

Merry casually struck him aside. "I must see your daughter."

"Never. I..."

"What is it, father?" A girl stood at a doorway. She clutched a thin robe about her, and even cynical Merry could recognise her natural, unspoiled beauty.

He bowed to her. "Is your name Jean?"

"It is. What do you want?"

Merry sighed. For the first time he doubted the wisdom of his mission. "Once you loved a man and he loved you. You must remember Gregg. Gregg Harmond."

She flushed. "Continue."

"He doesn't know that I'm here," Merry babbled. "He must never know; he'd kill me if he ever found out. He's a sick man. A very sick man, and I believe that you are the only one who could help him."

"How?"

"He has never forgotten you. Will you send him a message?"

"No. I can't. You mustn't ask me." She hid her face in confusion.

"He killed Owen," the oldster grated. "My son, your brother. Without him we are ruined. Our house burned, crops withered, poverty at every turn, all this he did."

"Nonsense," snapped Merry. "He didn't even know that Owen was aboard until it was too late. Alendi killed Owen, and Alendi is dead. Blame me if you must, but Gregg had nothing to do with it."

"Is that true?"

"On my oath, I swear it." Merry hoped that they didn't know how lightly he held his oath before. Now, when belief was essential, he doubted his ability to convince them.

The old man wasn't. He didn't want to be. For years he had lived with his fanatical hatred, and nothing would ever change his opinion. Jean was different.

"How is he?"

"At the crossroads," Merry snapped. "There is going to be a battle. Gregg may lose everything. Let me take him a crumb of comfort. Let me tell him that you, at least, he can reply on. Will you do this for him?"

"Get out!" the old man screamed. "Get out at once!"

Merry shrugged and moved towards the door. Jean followed him. "Tell him this," she murmured, "If he wants me, I'll be here, waiting."

The door thudded shut behind him, and Merry laughed into the brewing storm.

* * * *

Over the galaxy unrest stirred. Men felt the unease and looked to their possessions. Old ambitions blossomed anew. Forgotten wrongs suddenly clamoured for revenge. Greed stirred, and sheer desire for aggression.

Rulers of star-wide empires taxed and re-taxed their subjects. Trade became ringed with tariffs, tribute, plain graft. A thousand petty Lords tried to do the impossible and wring the last credit from their vassals. Men murmured, looked darkly, and fingered their weapons. Like a river, a golden tide, wealth showered on the Warbirds.

They were on sale to the highest bidder, and suddenly, through fear, hate, greed, every and anyone who thought he had something to gain or lose, wanted their services.

Wendle of the great Tri-Combine, looked dour and assembled his forces. Massine, grinned, and promised, and the Independents grew fat with easy spoil. Gregg promised nothing; but frantic would-be employers tried to sweeten the Eagles with gifts. They were accepted, and Fenson gloated.

"We're rich," he crowed. "The richest Warbirds ever to flap wing! Why, in hard cash alone, we're billionaires!"

"We were that before," said Gregg coldly. "Remember, we've got to earn that cash."

"So what?" Fenson shrugged. "We'll win. We always win."

"Maybe. But there's always a first time. Where's Merry?"

"Checking over the new flagship. Have you seen it yet?"

"No. Good, is it?"

"A beauty." Fenson smacked his lips. "Plenty of firepower, full radar protection, auxiliary life-craft, the works. With just one ship like that we could have beaten the entire Rim strength. With fifty we could beat the Galaxy."

"Well, we haven't got fifty," Gregg snapped irritably. "They cost too much. A ship like that is worth a whole planet."

"What of it?" Fenson looked at Gregg in surprise. "I've never known you to begrudge the cost of equipment before. Isn't it worth it?"

"When we can use it, yes. But what good is it otherwise? What good is any war machine if there is no war?"

Fenson chuckled. "There will be enough war soon to satisfy even you. We'll take on the Independents, beat them, and then wipe out the Tri-Combine. Then we'll run the Galaxy." He drew a deep breath. "Think of it—the first man to rule a universe! Doesn't it get you?"

"Yeah," Gregg said dully. "A wonderful ambition. If it works."

Fenson dropped his light tone of banter and moved closer. "Something troubling you, Gregg?"

"If the Independents and Tri-Combine unite, we'll be wiped out."

"You think that they will?

"No. Wendle doesn't trust Massine, but neither do I. I'd like to clear him out of the way. But I'm worried. Wendle has something up his sleeve. He's too sure of himself. As if the rest of us are doing exactly the things he wants us to do." He sighed, and left the table. "One thing I do know. We could never beat the Tri-Combine with our present strength."

"Couldn't we unite with the Amalgamated?"

Gregg laughed curtly. "I tried once. No. Massine would let us down. It would be suicide."

He glanced up as a knock came at the door. "Yes?"

"Radio message from the Lord of Botan, sir. Shall I connect your screen?"

"Yes."

Selid looked worriedly from the visi-screen and stared accusingly at Gregg. "Have you seen Selene?"

"Of course not. Why?"

Selid gestured wearily. "She has left the palace. Paul, too. I thought that you may have known something about it."

"No. I had nothing to do with it. We're ten light years from you, and have been here almost two weeks. When did they leave?"

"I'm not sure. I saw her two days ago. Paul has only recently recovered from his wound."

"Did they take a ship? Is one missing?"

"A light pleasure yacht. You think that they took it?" He frowned. "But why?"

"I don't know. Honeymoon, perhaps." He sounded bitter. "I'll do what I can do," he assured Selid. "If you hear of anything, let me know."

The screen darkened, blacking out the worried features of the Lord of Botan. Merry came bursting through the door. "What's the matter, Gregg?"

"Selene and Paul have disappeared. Nothing important."

"No?" Merry frowned. "I don't trust that pair, Gregg. You should have finished him off when he drew on you. I don't believe in leaving enemies—alive."

A siren clamoured throughout the ship. A metallic voice roared from hidden speakers. "Action stations! Action stations!"

The signal of attack!

* * * *

It was a single ship. Gregg cut off the action warning, and watched it in amazement. Guns followed its flight, ready to blast it from space at the first sign of danger, but none came. Gently, delicately balanced on flaming jets it settled, landed, and from an open port a loading ramp slid to the still smoking surface of the field.

"I think that it's a ship of the Independents. No insignia, but it's a war vessel right enough." Merry squinted through the port. "Wonder what they want?"

"We'll soon find out," said Gregg grimly. "Someone's coming over."

"We should blast them," Fenson grunted. "They asked for it, landing without permission." He hitched at his gunbelt. "I'll see who they are." He swung out of the room bawling orders.

Men ran from the clustered ships, surrounded the approaching pair. Others entered the newly-arrived vessel. Within minutes the Eagles had full command of the situation. Footsteps clattered on the metal flooring. Weapons clashed, someone knocked on the door.

"Two persons to see you, sir. Newly arrived and with messages from Massine."

"Enter."

The door swung wide, and Gregg stared into the eyes of Selene.

For a moment there was dead silence. She smiled a little tremulously, and took a step towards him.

"Gregg!"

He ignored her. "Search him for weapons," he ordered harshly. Paul flushed, but allowed the search without comment. "What are you doing here?"

"Gregg, will you help us? We ran away. My father couldn't understand, but we are in love, Gregg. Nothing matters but that." She shrugged. "My father thought that Paul wasn't good enough for me. I think that I'm not good enough for him."

"Why come to me?"

"Where else could we go, Gregg? Paul is ruined. You saw to that. He has only just recovered from his wound—the one you gave him." She stepped closer to him. "Once you said that you loved me, Gregg, and I thought that I loved you. If you meant what you said then, you will help us. If not..." She broke off, dabbing at her eyes.

Gregg turned to the radio operator. "Contact the prize crew." He waited while the connection was made. "Hello. Prize crew? Take the ship up. Swing into an orbit well above the atmosphere. Keep in radio contact. Any other personnel aboard?"

"None, sir."

"Right. Blast off. Conduct examination while in space."

Tubes thundered across the field. On a pencil of flame the little ship rose into the air, higher, higher, vanishing into the blackness of space. Selene turned white, clutching her throat. "Why did you do that?"

"You wanted help, didn't you? Well, you've got it. You may stay here at my base. Your ship was in the way. It can stay in orbit until we need it." He glanced at Paul. "Now, suppose you tell me just why you did come here?"

"Selene has told you."

"Does it take you two days to cover ten light years? And where did you get that ship?"

"From the palace landing field."

"Liar!" Gregg snarled the word, his face like granite. "You left Botan in a light yacht. You arrive days late in a warship—an old but a warship nonetheless. Where did you get it?"

"From the palace."

Gregg stepped forward, swung his hand savagely. The sound of the slap echoed through the room. "Talk, damn you!" he grated. "Or I'll turn you loose to those who will make you."

Something shook the ship. A dazzling burst of livid flame reached down from above, and heat seared the ground and ships. Men staggered and fell. Geiger counters chattered, and somewhere a man began screaming. Sound thundered down, then all was silent again.

Merry leaned against a wall wiping blood from his face. "Space!" he croaked. "Atom bombs!"

"The ship," gasped a man. "It was the ship."

Gregg turned to Paul, and something in his eyes made the arrogant, one-time Commander, shiver. "Don't, Gregg. I didn't know. I didn't know, I tell you!" His voice rose almost to a scream.

"They told us it would be bacterial. We were vaccinated, immune." Selene began to laugh. "They offered equal command. Full protection, the chance at an empire." Hysteria took charge of her. She collapsed, shrieking horribly. Gregg watched stonily as she was carried out.

"The Independents?"

"Yes." Paul seemed stunned with horror. "They would have killed us all."

"Take him away," snapped Gregg.

"Don't kill me," Paul pleaded. "Think of Selene."

"I'm thinking of my crew," snarled Gregg. "Don't worry. When you die, I'll kill you personally."

He stabbed a button. From the ship a siren began to wail a discordant note.

CHAPTER II

DECLARATION OF WAR

"They don't know but that their trap succeeded," explained Gregg. "They probably had a timing device to detonate the bomb a short while after landing. We were lucky. If Selid hadn't radioed me, I might have taken them at their face value. The Independents must know that the bomb detonated, but they can't know the actual damage. We'll attack while they are still in doubt."

Merry sucked at his lip. "Where do we attack first, Gregg?"

"Their home base. Massine has most of his strength assembled at the Lyrigian system; he owns several worlds there. We arrange with Selid to issue the challenge after we are assembled for attack. As soon as he has done it we dive in."

"Why issue challenges at all? Why not just blast the scum from the ether?" Fenson nursed a burnt shoulder and spat.

"Remember the Tri-Combine. We must play the game out at face value."

"What about them? Can they justify that bomb?"

"They don't have to. We've no evidence."

"No?" Fenson grinned savagely. "I could make those two squeal."

"Who'd believe them?" Gregg frowned. "No. We'll do it my way. Are the ships ready to go?"

Merry nodded. "Do we all go in at once?"

"No. You and Fenson will each be in Command of reserves. Stay out of the battle until I signal, or if I'm knocked out, when you think you're needed. I want to get Massine to concentrate his forces. A quick action. We can't mess about trying to wear them down with thoughts of using their captured ships. Smash them. Give them no chance to scatter." He passed a hand wearily across his forehead. "I don't know if any of us will get out of this alive. I'll say this now—if I'm killed, you'll find money put by in a reserve account. No matter what happens, you'll be rich."

Fenson snorted. "Why talk of dying? Hey! You there!"

"Yes, sir?" The uniformed aide saluted and stood smartly at attention.

"You'll find a couple of bottles in my cabin. Fetch them, with glasses."

Fenson nodded as the bottles were set before him, and jerked a thumb at the door. "Beat it." He lifted one, and snapped the neck on the edge of the table. Thick ruby wine flowed into the glasses.

"Strange," said Gregg, lifting his to the light. "Whenever we come to a climax in our lives, we always drink the wine of Prokeen."

"Seems a good idea," grunted Merry, wiping his lips. "It's always brought us luck."

Gregg toyed with his glass. "I'll always remember that planet. Warm, nice people, nice air." He sighed. "Better than Lagos. I think that if the people of Lagos could shift to Prokeen they would better for it. Not so cold, so hard." He drank, deeply of his wine.

"We started there," mused Fenson. "I wonder where we will end?"

"In hell, like as not," Merry grunted. "But it's been worth it, every step of the way." He drained his glass. "The devil with sentiment. We've a job ahead of us. Will you take the flagship, Gregg?"

"Yes, and a half of our total strength. You and Fenson each take a quarter. I'll lead the attack. You stand by above and below the plane of action. When I call, come with all guns working."

"Right." Merry stood up from the table. "I'll get ready. Coming, Fenson?"

"Sure." The ugly man hesitated a moment, then dropped one hand onto Gregg's shoulder. "Be seeing you, Gregg."

"Why not?" Gregg forced himself to smile. "We always win."

"That's the spirit." Fenson followed Merry out of the ship. At the foot of the loading ramp they paused, looking upwards.

"How do you feel, Merry?"

"How do you mean?" Merry squinted at Fenson. "How should I feel?"

"I don't know, but somehow this time it's different. Before, it was just another job. Now..." He shrugged. "I've got butterflies in my guts, like I did on my first action." He shivered. "I don't know how you feel, Merry, but I feel like hell."

He strode across the field towards his ships. Merry watched him until he disappeared around a towering bulk. He spat in the sand. "Like hell, eh?" he muttered. "So do I, Fenson. So do I."

Angrily he half ran towards his ships.

* * * *

Massine stared into the screen with undisguised amusement. Selid stared back in aloof dignity. He masked his feelings, but the Warbird's derision made him uneasy."

"Are you sure you want to fight?" Massine sneered.

"This is a formal declaration of war between myself and the Empire of Lyrigis. I understand that you are defender of that system. I speak for the Eagles."

"Oh? And why can't they speak for themselves?"

"Harmond agreed that I should issue the notice."

"When?"

"Yesterday." Selid frowned. "Really, I can't see why you shouldn't take my word for it. In any case the Eagles will attack three parsecs from the Lyrigian system. Co-ordinantes Z20/N15/D38."

"Agreed." Massine laughed again, and opened the circuit. "Reilly," he yelled.

"What is it?"

"Selid's issued a challenge. Prepare the fleet."

"Who're we up against?"

"Harmond's crowd—the Eagles."

Reilly's jaw dropped. "Hell, Massine, I don't know if the Captains will follow us this time. Harmond's got a hell of a reputation."

"Make 'em," Massine snarled. "Anyway, Harmond's dead. Selid didn't know about our little surprise. I bet the Eagles are a heap of rubbish. It'll be a walkover."

Reilly, a big, solid man in stained leather uniform, rubbed his jaw thoughtfully. "I'm not sure. The observation ship didn't report any secondary explosions, and photographic spectrographs seemed to indicate that the bomb exploded in outer space."

"So?" Massine bit his lip thoughtfully. "Where did Harmond originate? His home world, I mean."

"Rim planet called Lagos. Grim place by all account. The girl told us quite a bit about Harmond, not much of it useful."

"Selid's daughter, wasn't she?" Massine sat musing. "It's worth the chance. Detail a ship, an old, obsolete model will do, to load with radidust and head for Lagos."

"Radidust! Messine, are you crazy? You know that all radidusts are outlawed. If the Tri-Combine found out they'd blast us to atoms."

"They won't find out," Messine snarled. "Do as I say. If Harmond isn't dead it may be a useful bargaining point. No man wants to see his home world dusted. He might have a mother there, a sister, someone he cares for." He glared at Reilly. "Well, don't just stand there. Get that ship loaded and away."

"No." Reilly's jaw set stubbornly. "I won't do it. I've done a lot since I signed up with you, but I draw the line at dusting a planet."

"Hell, man, it'll only be bluff." Massine's lips writhed in an abortive smile. "Don't you see that?"

"Then why send a ship at all?"

"Because if we need to they can radio from Lagos itself, then he will know that we mean business." He stepped closer. "You know what will happen to you if we lose this engagement, don't you? You'll be a hobo, a tramp, scum of the spaceways. Nobody will want you; you'll starve. Now you've got your own ship, a steady income, women; everything you want. Do you want to throw it all away?"

Reilly grew thoughtful. "I guess not," he agreed.

"Good." Massine slapped his arm. "Now, just get that ship loaded and away. It's insurance, man—insurance against poverty." He grinned wickedly. "And hurry," he called after the man. "We blast off as soon as possible."

Scant hours after receiving the challenge, ships began to lift from home base. Sleek ships, bearing many insignia, but all bearing one in common. The bunched lightning flashes of the Independents. Massine sat in his flagships, and from all parts of the Centre ships received the call for aid. From a hundred far-flung worlds ships lifted spacewards. Grim, turreted, battle scarred. Manned by desperate men, who fought for fighting's sake, and who stood to lose everything they owned on this one final engagement.

* * * *

Deep in the immensity of space mighty engines of destruction moved to a common point. Ports masked, tubes silent, all electrical activity dead, they were undetectable. Aside from a faint shimmer of reflected starlight, nothing betrayed their presence. In the blackness of interstellar space they lurked like dead things, but they were far from dead.

Gregg sat at the control panel of the flagship and waited, every nerve tense. Behind him he could hear the whisper of the ranging officer scanning the vastness in which they moved.

"Object at Z5/N2/D8. Fore turrets align and follow. Object at Z4/N2/D6. Object at Z3/N2/D1. Object classified as meteor. Turrets range as 0/0/0."

Irritably Gregg switched off the running whisper from the ranging officer. Time enough for him to take a more active part. Now all he could do was wait.

His entire section of the fleet was moving closer to Massine's home worlds under momentum. Spread in a concave pattern he could concentrate all the fire-power of each ship onto a common point. Nothing known in space could last through such a bombardment.

Idly he thought of Selene. Strangely he didn't hate her. He had dropped her, together with Paul, on Botan as they passed through the system. Drugged for at least fifty hours they could do little harm. Either the trap worked, or they were in for the most desperate fight for all the long years of battling.

Thinking of Selene brought unwelcome thoughts of Jean. He wondered how she was getting on. Lagos was a hard world. Prokeen now... A flashing from the panel caught his attention.

"Objects sighted dead ahead, sir." The voice of the officer was tense with excitement.

"Good." Gregg switched on the closed instrument.

"Objects at 6/6/3/. Showing jet flashes. Approx. over one hundred. All turrets alert for firing data."

A soft-noted siren wailed through the ship. Men struggled in space suits, leaving face plates open until the last possible moment. Throughout the vessel a silent wave of emotion ran, almost tangible in its very intensity. Men braced themselves, took deep breaths, wiped hands suddenly clammy with sweat, and then were somehow calm.

Gregg reseated himself before the control panel. The suits were bulky and uncomfortable, but very necessary when a single shot could penetrate the hull, releasing air into the vacuum of space, and bringing certain death to unprotected bodies.

On the outside vision screen before him he could see tiny flashes of light, like a cloud of fireflies. They spread across the starry expanse—the jet flares of the enemy. Careless of discovery, it could mean only overwhelming confidence, or utter ignorance of the lurking forces ahead. Whatever it was they were in for a surprise.

Gregg smiled and spoke into his throat microphone. "All guns stand by. Alert and ranged. Wait for the command and then fire in salvo."

He settled down to wait.

A voice whispered in one ear. "Objects at 2/12/15. Flare trails of jets. Approx. fifty." Gregg closed a switch.

"Merry."

"Yes?"

"Watch ships to our right and above."

"You're covered."

The ship suddenly jerked, auxiliary jets flamed briefly then died. Guided missiles, ranging projectile, or just a meteor, it didn't matter. They had betrayed their position.

Gregg stabbed a button. "All guns. Fire!" The ship shuddered beneath the recoil. From the turrets livid gouts of flame blasted as ranging projectiles hissed to their targets. Guided missiles sprang from the launching tubes, leaving thin trails of fire from their rockets. For a split second nothing seemed to happen, then space ahead became brilliant with explosions.

Almost immediately came the answering fire. Gregg snapped orders into the throat mike, and the ships veered, altered course, slid through space at erratic intervals of time and distance. Around them searing explosions ripped, filling space with incandescent gases, and semi-molten metal.

Continually the guns belched forth their cargoes of destruction. From the ships ahead flared mushrooms of smoke-fringed flame. Bursting into eye-searing brilliance, then dying through expansion to a sullen, glowing cloud of gas. Each such display marked the end of an enemy by direct hit. The atomic piles in the engine rooms had given way, and radiation had blasted the area clean of all living things.

More frequent were the minor casualties. Hulls ripped, turrets burst open, men torn and maimed by the fury of jagged steel. Such a battle could go on for days, each side standing back and fighting with long-range missiles. Gregg wanted to finish it quick. He had to. He leaned forward towards his panel.

"All ships full speed ahead. Eccentric passage. Get in close and rip their guts out!"

He felt the surge of power as the ship flung itself forward. His fingers itched to grasp the smooth metal of a turret gun, but he restrained himself. Trained men sat in those turrets. He would be needed later.

The fleets drew nearer. Now it was possible to see them clearly through the ports with the unaided eye. Grim vessels, scattered widely throughout the region. As they drew close the real battle began. Close range guns spewed blasts of pure heat. Turret blasters seared and burnt the hulls, misted the ports, melted the sprouting guns. For a while, chaos seemed to rule, each ship firing with every weapon they carried.

Space grew bright with shed energy, and starlight gleamed from twisted wreckage.

A voice crackled from Gregg's ear. "Need us yet?"

"Not yet, Fenson. Merry?"

"Yes?"

"Spot any ships anywhere near us?"

"A group coming at you from 12/12/50. Shall I take them?"

"Not yet. If we can smash these first all the better. Wait until the others join the action then rip into them."

Something smashed against the hull. The lights flickered, died. Emergency lights glowed dully. Gregg dizzily climbed to his feet. Something wet ran down his face, but the face-plate of his helmet prevented his feeling for the wound.

Another blow knocked him to the floor. Air puffed from the control room. An aide, attempting to help Gregg to his feet, suddenly slumped, a jagged hole in his back. Gregg fought his way to the intership radio.

"Fire room. What's the damage?"

"Fore turrets out. Mid turrets erratic. Rest O.K."

"Can we break free of action?"

"Maybe."

"Get free if possible. Use long range weapons until damage repaired." He called Merry. "Those ships arrived yet?"

"Didn't you feel them? They joined action minutes ago."

"Get in here. The water's lovely. Fenson!"

"Yes?"

"Spread your ships. Individual fire. Take chances. We've got to finish this as soon as possible."

"Right. You O.K., Gregg?"

"Sure. Let's have some action."

The ship reeled beneath another blow.

CHAPTER 12

FORCE SCREEN

The firing died. The luminous clouds of flaming gases dulled, cooled, and expanded into vacuum. From the control room of the battered flagship, Gregg stared with bloodshot eyes at the visi-screen before him.

Massine snarled animal-like in his feral hate. Thin lips writhed and fingers twitched, yet for all his cursing, he knew that he was beaten.

"Harmond. I want to bargain with you. Do you think much of Lagos?"

"What?" Gregg frowned dully. His head hurt, and it was hard to think. "What about Lagos?"

"I want my life, Harmond. A ship, and all I own. If I don't get it, then Lagos will be dusted."

"Do you surrender?"

"I'm beaten, if that's what you mean. You can do as you like with the rest of the Independents, but what about me? Do we make a deal?"

"No."

"What?" Massine looked his surprise. "Don't you understand what I'm saying? Lagos will be a desert. All life extinct. I've got a ship loaded with radidust in orbit. At my signal they will shed the load. You know what that means!"

"What of it? What is Lagos to me? Yield, Massine, or I'll blast you to atoms."

"No, Gregg, no!" It was Merry. He with Fenson had been brought to the flagship by auxiliary rocket at the finish of the action. He lay on a stretcher, his uniform torn and burnt. Medics bent over him trying to stem the blood pouring from a shattered left arm. He pushed them away.

"You can't let him do it, Gregg. I've been there. Jean is waiting for you. She loves you, Gregg. You can't let her die." He fell back, exhausted.

Massine grinned. "Makes a difference, doesn't it? Well?"

Something appeared in the screen. A man, leather uniform ripped, bloodstained, black with smoke and fire. Eyes stared half-crazily from a seared face. He had caught a spent flare-gun charge, weak, but still strong enough to roast the living flesh. Reilly swayed, caught the edge of the screen, and laughed.

"Trying to bluff you, Harmond!" He staggered. "I heard you, Massine. Selling us out, eh? Well, I can stop that." He thrust his face towards the screen. "Don't worry, Harmond. That ship..." He groaned and fell. Massine grinned savagely, and holstered the weapon.

"Well, Harmond? Time's getting short. Do I dust Lagos, or not?"

He grinned, then his face changed. The thin lips writhed, twisted; he screamed and spun from the screen. From his back the hilt of a knife showed clear against the green uniform. Reilly's voice came weakly from the screen, "Don't worry. I loaded the ship. Not radidust. Not..." A gurgle, and silence.

Merry sighed, and muttered with pain. Fenson wiped his face, and stared stupidly at the blood on his hand. Gregg slumped in the control seat and nursed a blood-caked temple.

Suddenly, with shocking abruptness, sirens wailed the alarm throughout the ship.

"Action stations! Action stations! Fleet approaching. Action stations!"

Gregg sat numb. Another attack. With sickening realisation he knew that the Eagles were in no condition to battle. They were beaten before they could ever start!

* * * *

The ships ringed them, grim in their turreted sleekness. Guns menaced them, but as yet no shots had been fired. Gregg stared into the screen and frowned in puzzlement.

"I don't recognise the insignia. Do you, Fenson?"

"Looks like a flaming comet. No, I can't place it. No other Wargroup that I know of in this part of the Galaxy."

"They wish to make contact, sir." A tattered officer lifted his head from the radio.

"Connect the screen."

"They wish for personal contact. Ask for permission to board. What shall I reply, sir?"

Gregg laughed curtly. "Have we any choice? Let them board." A slight bump as the auxiliary rocket touched the hull. Heavy footsteps of space-suited men. The control room door swung open. Men entered, slipped out of their suits. Stood upright.

Gregg stared with amazement, then despite his weariness, grinned. "Hello, Wendle. Welcome to the Eyrie." He sagged. "I didn't recognise you. Your insignia, even your uniform. Why did you change?"

"The Tri-Combine is dead. As dead as the Amalgamated, the Independents—yes, as the Eagles." He seemed very grave. The thin features, lined and scarred, wreathed with the thin, white hair, seemed different, as if he had lost his cynicism and had found something far better.

He wore a black uniform, almost identical to that worn by Gregg and his Eagles. The piping was of silver, and the insignia was a flaming comet, otherwise they were the same.

"What happened to you?"

"I grew up, Gregg." The old voice was calm and certain. "I've wanted to for a long time, and you gave me the chance. I am grateful for that." He paused, and sat down. He looked at Merry. "Bad?"

"It's his arm, sir," answered one of the medics, respectfully. "It's badly shattered. I'm afraid that we'll have to amputate."

"A pity." His voice was calm. "There has been much bloodshed. Now it is over."

"What do you mean?" Gregg stirred from his sat. "What are you going to do?"

Wendle gestured towards the screen. "You see that ship out there? I want you to fire at it. Or pick any one you choose."

Gregg stared hard at him. "Seeking an excuse to wipe us out, Wendle?"

"No. I want to show you something. Go ahead. Pick a ship and blast it!"

Gregg shrugged, and leaned across the control panel.

"Gunnery officer? Pick a target and fire with all guns." He listened for a moment. "I mean it. Concentrate all fire on one target." A silence, then the ship shook under the recoil of all guns.

They watched the target in the screen. None of the shots reached it. The ship shook again and again. Fire splashed, rebounded, hid the ship. It cleared, and the target was unharmed.

Gregg spun to face Wendle. "A trick?"

"No. A force screen." He sighed. "Did you think that the Arsenal ever sold you the latest in weapons? Why should they? They had their own plans, and so did I. The force screen makes them possible. The Warbirds, the mercenary Groups living on strife, are finished. They served their purpose, but now they are unnecessary—and unwanted."

"So the Tri-Combine wins the Galaxy?" Gregg sounded bitter.

"No. Not the Tri-Combine. The Galactic Patrol!" Pride rang in his voice. "With the force screen we are undefeatable. And that same force screen makes us the natural guardians of the Universe. The Tri-Combine has the ships, the organisation, and the trained personnel. We are talking over. A small levy on each habitable world, proportionate to trade and population, will suffice to make the patrol self-sufficient."

Gregg nodded understandingly. "I see," he sighed. "Of all endings, this I least expected. The Warbirds seemed settled, a part of civilisation, a logical part. Space is too big to patrol. Too many worlds have their petty grievances. The Warbirds took care of them. Bloodless war. Bloodless from a civilian's viewpoint, that is. They only paid."

He looked at Wendle. "I served your purpose, didn't I? The Eagles cut down all opposition, leaving their forces intact. You played a crafty game, Wendle, but I don't blame you for it. I would have done the same."

Wendle smiled. "Don't feel too bad about it. I could have blasted you from space, but I didn't."

"Why not?"

"Is it necessary? Massine recorded a conversation he had with you when you attacked the Amalgamated. We monitored it. Somehow I don't think that you are too displeased with the way things have turned out."

Gregg shrugged. "I suppose not. What will happen to the Eagles?"

"Nothing." Wendle smiled again. "We don't intend ruining you. If Massine had won, it would have different. We would have wiped him out, but I think that we can trust you."

"For what?"

"Patrolling the Rim."

"No." Gregg shook his head. "I don't want that. I've had enough of ships and guns and fighting. This is the end for me. I've seen too much blood."

"Then why not bury the Eagles? Strip your ships of armament, convert them to trade, passenger service, anything. You have an organisation, the Rim needs ships and men. With your wealth, you would bring a flood of prosperity to the Rim which would be the stabilising of the colonies there. Well?"

Gregg smiled. "I'll put it to the men, but I know what I'll do." He touched the insignia on his breast. "I think I'll keep this—as a trademark."

"Good." Wendle stood up. Suddenly he held out his hand. "From the first Commander of the Galactic Patrol, to the last and greatest of the Warbirds, thank you. I am glad, very glad, that it was you who won."

Gregg took the proffered hand. He suddenly felt very glad that things had worked out this way.

* * * *

A woman stood at the door of a roughly fashioned log house, and stared eagerly towards the edge of town. She was tall, with a proud beauty, though sorrow had left its mark in tiny lines around her eyes, and a saddened expression on her oval face.

The winter had passed, and spring had come to Lagos. A bad winter it had been, but now she smiled and had hope again.

Two men came striding through the mud towards her. One was tall, lithe, with an ugly scar marring one temple. The other was still fat, and wore an empty sleeve on his left side.

Gregg stepped forward. "Jean," he said huskily. "Merry told me. I'm so terribly glad that you waited."

"Gregg," she said. Then again, "Gregg."

"How is your father?"

"He died, Gregg. Times were hard, and he caught an infection." She smiled. "He was old, and very bitter. But he was a good man, Gregg. He did what he thought was right." She held out her hand to Merry. "I'm glad that you're alive. Was the battle very terrible?"

Merry chuckled. "Not as bad as some I've seen, but bad enough." He flapped his sleeve. "About time the Warbirds settled down. A one-winged Eagle isn't much use in a battle."

He smiled at them both. "I suppose that you will be getting married now. Well, about time, too, I'd say. Gregg hasn't been human these past few years." His face softened. "Be kind to him, Jean. He's a good man."

"What are you going to do?" she asked. "We won't have much, but you are welcome to share."

Merry looked at her in amazement. "Do you think we're ruined, girl?" He laughed. "Why, every man who wore the Eagle is rich." He chuckled again.

"Thank you for your kind thoughts, though." He squinted at the sky. "I'll be getting along now, Gregg. Mind you fetch your wife to Prokeen for the honeymoon. There is a wine-shop keeper there that I intend making the richest woman in this part of the Rim." He sighed. "Fenson has the same idea, so I daren't linger. I've lost an arm, but he's lost an ear, and is ugly as sin, to boot. Still, it'll be a fair match."

They watched him stride down the road towards the landing field. "Are you really rich, Gregg?"

"Yes, darling. Merry wasn't lying. My ship is at the field. Does it matter?"

She smiled and shook her head. He stepped closer to her, and automatically his arms went about her. "Jean!"

"Gregg!"

Their lips met.